BEHIND THE GATES

Charisse Peeler

To Patricia and Marissa who inspired me to write this book during one of our many adventures and to my husband Mike who is my biggest fan and the love of my life.

CHAPTER 1

Green Tea Shot

The air was thick inside O'Malley's. The ancient air handler was losing its battle against the heavy August night in Boca Raton. The brick-faced building, originally a firehouse, had long ago been converted into a unique bar and grill serving as the local watering hole. It was also the closest place to the gated community of Banyan Tree Country Club where the younger members could have a drink after six p.m.

The old fire truck doors of the original building remained intact, and tonight they had been thrown wide open, allowing the Wednesday-night crowd of patrons to spill out onto the pavement—more room on which to enjoy the $1 wings featured on the midweek menu.

On Wednesday nights, too, O'Malley's hosted the local dart league.

The Boca Boozers was one of the teams that gathered once a week to throw sharp plastic-tipped shafts at the black-and-red dartboards while standing behind an officially measured twenty-four-inch line of tape on the floor. The tape marked a horizontal distance of exactly seven feet, nine and one-quarter inches from the board. If there was a technique to throwing a dart, it included the player placing one foot in front of the other while still remaining behind the line of tape, leaning his (or her) torso across the line as far as possible—elbow up, one eye closed—then tossing the dart with a nice, smooth release.

Marco Escobar was usually a stickler for the rules—and one of the best players on Boca Boozers. But tonight he didn't care. He stood from the Boozers' table to line up his throw. Only, instead of lining up he turned to the waitress and helped himself to one of the green tea shots she carried confidently on her tray. He downed the light green concoction, closed one eye, then threw his last dart, missing the board completely—and thereby causing the opposing team to erupt in cheers. "Boca Boozers, no longer undefeated!" some guy from the other team crowed mockingly.

The waitress distributed the remaining green tea shots to Marco's teammates. Marco reached over and swiped one of the glasses from out of his teammate's hand, but he didn't care. It was a shit day…he wasn't in the mood for games. He put the shot glass down before weaving through the crowd, stumbling out the door and tripping over to the side of the building, where his golf cart was parked. Marco had been drinking since noon: he was a bit wobbly on his feet. In any case it was a relief to get out of the crowded bar, which had been putting him in a worse mood than he had already been in before he stepped inside.

Thunder rumbled in the dark sky. A flash of lightning in the near distance threatened rain, typical in South Florida this time of year. Marco didn't care. He took his time driving down the sidewalk, cruising just a few blocks to the back gate of the country club. He would wait here until someone drove in or out and the gate opened; then he would piggyback through.

A different world lay behind these gates. Different from the world Marco was used to anyway. People behaved differently here. This was a life he thought would be perfect. At first, he had enjoyed the two beautiful golf courses and the camaraderie of the guys at the card table, but it was the rules that frustrated him the most. One thing Marco didn't like was to be told what to do.

As he sat in his golf cart next to the gate, hoping to beat

the imminent deluge, his head filled with the frustrations of the day, especially the latest letter he had received from the board. He was facing yet another grievance, and possibly more time restricted from the golf course. The longer he waited by the gate the angrier he became…He vowed that everyone who had testified against him at the last board meeting would pay for their troubles.

Finally, the bar rose and the gate slowly opened, releasing a dark Cadillac SUV from the compound. As soon as the vehicle was past the bar, Marco weaved his golf cart around the wide-eyed octogenarian, who visibly shook in surprise.

Marco laughed. "Go ahead and turn me in, you old fart," he yelled. He knew chances were he wouldn't get turned in. One reason: there really wasn't any rule against it. He knew this because he had memorized the entire membership rules and regulations for the country club. The guy probably didn't know who he was anyway. His golf cart had no identifying marks, primarily because of the club's stupid rule that every golf cart had to be the exact same color…never mind the fact that Marco made sure to cover up his membership number whenever he drove the golf cart off the property.

The most efficient way back home would have been to take a right on Banyan Tree Lane. But Marco's brain was devious tonight, and he decided to detour through the golf course. He took his phone out and pushed the button to activate the phone's camera. He would ride by the board members' homes, hoping to record some violation, even though the night was probably too dark at this point to be worth it. But these were his sworn enemies: he would figure out a way to pay them back for all the crap they put him through. His revenge couldn't be too obvious or be able to be attributed to him. What he really needed was an accomplice…and he knew exactly where to find one.

Marco drove past the clubhouse. He had been banned from its confines for the next six weeks because of a few ridiculous transgressions—he doubted if any of the board members could even remember what they were. But just as he drove past, Rodney stumbled out the back door, bungling his way into the crowded area where all of the golf carts were lined up. Rodney had been enjoying the clubhouse's convivial offerings for a while, obviously. His normal carefully combed hair was mussed, and half his shirt was untucked. Marco stopped in his path. He parked right behind Rodney's golf cart and waited until he was close enough to speak.

"Hey, Marco," Rodney said in his heavy South African accent.

"Wanna join me for a nightcap?" Marco asked.

"Sure," Rodney replied. "A nightcap sounds good but I need to stop home first."

Marco pulled out and let Rodney back up then lead the way along several golf paths until they reached Ibis Lane. The golf course was dark, the roads were quiet. Rodney clicked the door opener to his garage. His 1972 bright yellow Corvette, painstakingly restored, and his 2018 white 435 BMW convertible with the red interior were parked side by side.

Marco parked his golf cart in the driveway, right next to Rodney's. He followed Rodney through the interior garage door, past the laundry room and into the living room, where he took a seat in one of Rodney's overstuffed leather chairs. The chairs faced the large sliding glass doors that looked out at the pool.

Marco liked Rodney. They had become friends on the golf course; but whenever Marco needed a sidekick Rodney was willing and able.

Rodney disappeared into the back of the house. A minute later Marco heard a toilet flush and water running. As he looked toward the hall, expecting Rodney to appear, he noticed an unfamiliar accessory hanging on the wall.

"Well, what is *this*?" Marco said. He climbed out of the overstuffed chair and moved to the object. "Is this a crossbow...?"

He reached up and removed the bow from its hook on the wall. He had never seen one before. It was triggered like a rifle but the string was split with a mechanism that pulled back the arrow. He whistled at the beautiful wood, then he felt its heft. He was like a kid with a new toy.

Rodney returned. He had changed from his pink golf shirt into a button-down Tommy Bahama.

"This is cool, man," Marco said.

Rodney nodded. "My brother sent it to me from South Africa."

"You can send this kind of shit in the mail?"

"I don't know." Rodney shrugged. "He did."

"Does it work?"

Again Rodney said, "I don't know."

"I think"—Marco said, smiling broadly—"we're about to find out."

"Then we'll need these." Rodney opened a side closet and pulled out a long box.

"Arrows?" Again Marco smiled. "Can't forget those…"

"*Bolts,*" Rodney corrected, using the proper term. But the next moment he decided to just forget it.

Marco tucked the crossbow under his arm and headed for the door. He climbed into his golf cart and drove over to his place, forgetting about Rodney until he pulled into his driveway. He parked his golf cart next to his old banged-up work truck, which was illegally parked in the driveway.

Following Marco, Rodney kept his foot heavy on the pedal then pulled into the driveway and parked behind Marco. He followed his friend through the house, and together they went into the backyard.

Marco flipped on his back lights. The powerful floods were so bright his yard felt like a stage at the local community theater. The association had no rules regarding lights, even though Marco's neighbors across the golf course had lodged a complaint that the light from Marco's yard was filtering into their bedroom. "*Buy some damn curtains,*" Marco had told them.

"Give me one of those arrows," Marco told Rodney now.

Rodney opened the long box. He carefully pulled out one

of the bolts and handed it to Marco. "What are you aiming at?" he asked.

It took Marco a couple minutes to properly load the arrow into the mechanical configuration. When he finally managed to get the weapon loaded, he held it up, aiming toward the golf course.

"See that tree across the golf course?"

"Yeah."

"Watch this…."

Marco pulled the trigger. The arrow flew quietly through the air as it disappeared into the darkness. Then Marco pointed to the countertop on the patio behind them. "Grab that flashlight, and give me another arrow."

Rodney handed him the arrow. Marco reloaded the bow. This time he put his eye purposefully to the scope and tweaked its height. Rodney pointed Marco's flashlight toward the tree Marco seemed to be aiming at. Marco pulled the trigger. The two men watched the bolt disappear in the bushes a few feet beyond the tree Marco had pointed out before.

Marco reloaded and tried a third time. This time he buried the bolt into the tree; but the bolt wouldn't be retrieved very easily: it had pierced the tree at least twenty feet above the base of the trunk.

With his ego in check, Marco handed the crossbow to Rodney.

"Do you want to try?"

"Nah, I need another drink," Rodney said. He walked back into the house, carrying the crossbow and the last bolt in his arms. He placed them carefully on the end of the kitchen counter.

"Make one for me," Marco yelled through the open door.

Satisfied, he sat calmly down in a lounge chair under the overhang.

"Will do," Rodney yelled back.

Just then Marco's sister, Angie, came out of her room.

Angie had moved in with Marco several months ago, trading the mental abuse and threatening behavior of her husband for the temper tantrums of her brother. She reminded herself daily that living with Marco was a temporary arrangement: she was willing to put up with it only until she had enough money to pay for the divorce.

Angie was wearing her work attire—black polyester pants and a white tux shirt. She pulled her long black hair back with one hand, her other hand twisting a black scrunchy around it and tying it into a ponytail.

"Going to work?" Rodney asked.

"What do you think?" Angie rolled her eyes.

"You know..."

"Not in a million years," Angie said.

"I didn't even say..."

"You were about to."

"If you would give me a chance, you would..."

"Rodney, if you were the last man on earth and I was the last woman and the future of humankind depended on us, I still would rather jump into a live volcano than live the rest of my life listening to your bullshit."

Angie grabbed her purse and slammed the front door as she left.

Rodney grabbed the drinks and joined Marco outside. "What's up with her?" he asked.

"She is *never* going out with you," Marco said.

"I don't know why not. If she gave me a chance, she wouldn't have to go to that shit job of hers. I would take care of her."

"She likes her shit job."

"Tell me she likes dealing cards to a bunch of idiots."

"She deals high rollers. Last night one of those 'idiots' gave her a hundred-dollar tip."

"Well, she could at least go on one date with me."

"My sister is only forty years old. What are you? Like, sixty-five?"

"I'm only sixty-two. Plus, age doesn't matter," Rodney

said. "Do I look sixty-two?"

"I was being generous when I said sixty-five," Marco said.

"Come on, man," Rodney said.

"I got another letter," Marco said, changing the subject.

"Oh God, serious? What did you do this time?"

"I didn't do anything. I'm telling you, these guys got it out for me."

"When is the hearing?"

"Next week…but you can help me out of this one," Marco said.

"What do you need me to do?"

Rodney stood up and walked back to the bar, filling his glass with ice and Grey Goose.

"Just bring the bottle," Marco yelled through the door.

Rodney grabbed the ice bucket and the bottle of vodka then set everything down on the small table between the two lounge chairs.

"What is the grievance and who filed it?"

"Just read the letter."

Marco pulled a folded piece of paper from his front pocket and handed it to Rodney before refilling his glass.

"You threatened Alan Sheffield?" Rodney asked.

"That's what he's claiming but there were no witnesses. And I didn't threaten him, exactly."

"Maybe not. But it says here you told him to be careful if he came home one night not to trip on his dead dog." Rodney gazed sternly at his friend. "Seriously Marco, were you going to kill his dog?"

"Jesus, no, Rodney, you know I would never hurt an innocent animal."

"Why would he make that up?" Rodney asked.

"I don't know. The guy hates my guts. I don't know why he has it in for me. If I spit on the sidewalk, I'd get another month suspension. It's ridiculous."

"So, what do you need me to do?"

"You just show up at the board meeting next Tuesday at

five o'clock and say you were standing close by and heard the whole conversation—I never said anything about a dead dog. I mean, you can make it believable, you can say I was raising my voice. What I actually said was that it wasn't fair that I've been under a microscope since the day I moved in here. They've been looking for any violation they can pin on me to get me mad enough to move out. Guess what? That isn't going to happen. The only way I'm leaving this club is in a body bag."

"A little dramatic there, Marco, but don't worry, I can come up with something."

Rodney leaned back and closed his eyes. He was drunk. The breeze created by the fan above his head…the rhythm of the turning blades…was just too much. He began to snore.

"Hey man, wake up!" Marco pushed Rodney's shoulder. He wanted to tell Rodney, *Just keep it simple.*

Rodney didn't wake up. Nonetheless Marco was relieved that Rodney had agreed to back up his story in front of the board. So he left him asleep outside while he went back into the house. The big bag of cat food sitting on the kitchen counter reminded him that he hadn't fed the cats today. He poured three big bowls and walked out the front door then set the bowls under the eaves at the side of the house. As soon as he set the bowls down, several neighborhood strays appeared, heading straight for the food.

Marco had started feeding the strays almost a year ago. Soon after the older woman across the street had died, he had overheard a member of the board mentioning that now some of the cats might disappear. So, for the price of some dry cat food, Marco had continued to drive the board crazy.

The most difficult part of taking revenge, Marco had learned over the years, was keeping quiet about it. He wanted his targets to know he was responsible, but at the same time he had to walk that fine line between getting suspended from the club and getting arrested.

He stood under the eaves for a few minutes, watching a few more cats arrive; then he went back into the house. As soon as he reached the kitchen, a chill ran down his spine. He looked around the house: some of the papers on his desk had been moved. Then he noticed the back door was wide open. He was sure he had closed it when he had come in earlier.

Rodney's snoring was unbearable. Marco again closed the slider, but when he turned back toward the kitchen, he was thrown backward by a force that took the breath out of him. His hands flew to his chest…where he promptly felt an arrow shaft buried deep into his bone. He fell to the floor, unable to breathe as he looked around for his attacker. Finally he saw the person holding the crossbow. He couldn't believe it. With his last breath he asked, "Why?"

*

Rodney came slowly out of his deep sleep; Angie's screaming had awoken him. He was so used to his own ex-wife screaming that he was numb to Angie's cries. He took his time getting out of the lounge chair. His head was throbbing from the vodka, and he had to pee; but instead of facing Angie inside, he used the eucalyptus hedges on Marco's patio to relieve himself.

The last thing he remembered from the night before was Marco saying something about a dead dog. Angie's screaming didn't stop—it was *so* loud. What time was it anyway, he wondered. He pulled open the sliding glass door. Inside, he saw Angie on her knees, pulling on the shaft of a bolt sticking out of Marco's chest. The sun hadn't quite made it over the horizon. The only light was a soft orange glow that made the entire scene confusing.

"Call 911, you moron!" Angie screamed.

Rodney searched his pockets until he located his phone. He wiped the drool from the side of his mouth. He still wasn't fully awake when the operator came on. When she asked the nature of his problem, he said, "I'm not sure but I think he's dead."

"Who's dead?" the operator asked.

"Marco."

"What is his last name, sir?"

"Escobar."

"Is he breathing?"

"I don't know." Rodney looked at Angie. "Is he breathing?"

"No, he's not breathing. He's got a fucking arrow in his chest!" Angie screamed.

"Sir… Sir…" The operator was trying to get Rodney's attention.

"No, he's not breathing," Rodney said into the phone. "I'm pretty sure he's dead. There's a bolt—an arrow—sticking out of his chest."

"Okay sir, I have a deputy dispatched to your location. I need you to stay on the phone with me until they get there."

"Okay."

"Sir, do you know what happened?"

"I was asleep," Rodney replied.

"Do you have anything to do with this sir?" the operator asked.

"I don't think so."

"Who is there with you?"

"His sister, Angie."

"Where is Angie?"

"Trying to pull the arrow out of his chest."

"Sir, tell her to move away from the body."

"Angie, they said move away from the body."

Angie sat back on her heels, her hands covered in blood. She wiped them on her black pants, but it didn't help. The blood merely spread farther up her arms.

"Sir… are there any weapons in the house?"

Rodney looked around. He spotted the crossbow on the counter, close to where he had set it the night before.

"Yes," he said.

"Okay, the deputies are just a few minutes away. Just hold tight."

It wasn't even five minutes later when the doors burst in from all sides and officers entered, guns drawn.

"Hands up!" demanded a loud voice.

Both Rodney and Angie reached up.

Rodney sat in the back of the Palm Beach County sheriff's car, watching the sky turn the most magical colors of orange and red. He breathed deeply, remembering when he first moved to Boca...how different it was from New York, but how similar to his home in South Africa.

Angie sat in a separate sheriff's vehicle. She had watched her brother's body, wrapped in a black zippered body bag, being loaded into an ambulance. She could see the rise in the middle, where the arrow was still lodged.

She didn't cry but kept her jaw clenched tight, wondering where she was going to live now. She worried whether she would be able to get her clothes and makeup, and would she be able to make it to work tonight?

By midmorning, the yellow police tape surrounding the perimeter of Marco's house on Iguana Lane had put the country club on full alert. A steady stream of golf carts slowly drove by, hoping to get a peak of the goings on. One by one, the residents questioned the officers, hoping to learn a bit of information they could share with their neighbors; but the officers gave the same answer to everyone who asked: "It's too early to tell."

Normally an ambulance in this neighborhood wasn't that big of a deal; the average age of the country club's residents was close to eighty. But the fact that it was Marco's house—and that Rodney had been spotted sitting in the back of a police car—created a bigger stir than might otherwise have been expected.

Both the front and back gates had local police checking cars and questioning residents. All of the contractors, pool cleaners, and landscapers were all turned away for the day to preserve any evidence that might have remained after the heavy rains that had fallen during the night. The golf staff were already fielding calls in regard to the yellow tape surrounding the trunk of the large banyan tree and nearby bushes on hole Number 4 of the lower course: an arrow was sticking out high amid the banyan's thick branches.

"If my ball lands inside the barrier, can I retrieve it?" was a common question from the golfers.

The answer from the staff was, "No."

"If it's close enough to the barrier, can I use a club or my retriever to reach in and get it?"

"No."

"So, where is the drop, then?"

"Is your ball inside the yellow tape?"

"No."

"Seriously these people don't live in reality."

CHAPTER 2

Moscow Mule

The breakfast crowd at the Tiki Grill reminded Maggie more of her high school lunchroom than the informal dining experience at the country club. Every morning the same cliques gathered at their regular tables. The jocks. The nerds. The ambitious wannabes in student government. The packs of mean girls. And, of course, the misfits.

Maggie, Alexandria, and Britney considered themselves members of the misfits: they were not traditional members at the club. There were two jock tables, the guys and the girls. The guys were the good golfers, and the girls were golfers and tennis players. The nerds were not really nerds but more loners who enjoyed turning through the staid, sober pages of *The Wall Street Journal* or the latest nonfiction hardback instead of the drama that was the necessary consequence of being in the company of others. The student government was the table of board members and the chairs of important committees. The mean girls didn't usually come to breakfast—but you could always be assured of finding them in the women's card room.

Whenever a new member arrived, the three women would guess what breakfast table they would join. Alexandra was usually right. Actually, she was right Every. Single. Time. Her expertise was likely due to her ability to read people; that, combined with her thirty-plus years of country club living.

Maggie poured herself a cup of coffee before she sat down with Alexandra and Britney.

"Did you hear?" Alex asked before Maggie even had the chance to sit.

"Hear what?"

"Marco is dead," Britney said.

Maggie stared at her incredulously. "You've got to be kidding."

"Not kidding," Alex replied.

"How?"

"Someone said Rodney shot him with a bow and arrow," Britney said.

Maggie scoffed. "That's crazy, Rodney just seems so mild mannered. I can't see him shooting anyone." She shook her head. "He wouldn't even know how to *shoot* a bow and arrow."

"You should know, you're the one who dated him." Britney flashed her friend a smile.

"Seriously?" Maggie replied. "I never dated him. We hung out a few times."

"Well that's not what he says," Alex observed.

"Maybe it was an accident?" Britney suggested, after a moment. "They had him in the back of a cop car."

In truth, it had been Alex who had brought the three women together. She had seen Britney siting alone at the bar one night and introduced herself, offering her friendship. Soon after, Maggie moved in. The three had been inseparable ever since. They had been brought together by a need for allies in the crazy world that existed behind the gates of the Banyan Tree Country Club. Their method of coping with the country club lifestyle was similar to the strategies necessary for surviving a natural disaster like a hurricane, or a medical emergency, like having to share a kidney. Country club life didn't quite suit them, but the Banyan Tree's community was where they chose to live.

Britney was the youngest of the group. She had just

turned twenty-nine and moved in two years ago. She was gorgeous—*absolutely* gorgeous!—as well as smart. Most of the people at the club assumed she was a high-end stripper or a trust fund baby living on her daddy's money. The first time she showed up at the country club's bar, she was met with side glances and turned-up noses. The ladies instantly hated her... and the men all wanted to get to know her better.

In truth, Britney was a self-made woman. Only five years prior, she had approached a small boutique hotel on Palm Beach Island, offering to redesign their lobby for a school project. It had proved to be her big break. She did such a great job on the lobby, the owners hired her as their exclusive designer for all their hotels. Soon she was so busy flying all over the country, she dropped out of her school and started her own company designing high-end hotel lobbies.

Maggie moved into the country club just a few months after Britney. She was a retired technical writer for Boeing in a suburb of Seattle, where she had spent her entire life. After a bitter divorce and the nonstop rain and grey skies, the fifty-five-year-old needed a new life somewhere less depressing.

Maggie had always wanted to write a novel. She had started several projects, but they didn't really go anywhere. She figured a new location would help inspire her; so she packed her bags and moved to Boca Raton.

Simply put, Alexandra was a class act. She was a part-time resident at the country club. No one knew her age; nor did they attempt to guess. When she lost her husband nearly four years ago, she also lost most of her friends. Whether this was because most of the activities were designed for couples or the wives didn't want a beautiful available woman around their husbands, she became an outcast. She wasn't ready to join the unofficial single women's club where all the women who had lost their husbands banded together and complained about their lives. She still had a life to live.

Alexandra was the current CEO of a midsize manufacturer of airplane parts in upstate New York, where she was born and raised. Now she commuted back and forth from Rochester to Boca Raton on her corporate jet. Her sweet smile and fashionable style were very deceiving. The lady stood four feet, nine inches tall. She might easily be confused for a retired kindergarten teacher with an amazing golf swing, but she was one tough cookie you didn't want to cross.

The three women sat at the four-top near the side door in order to have a full view of the morning's activities.

"Who found the body?" Britney asked.

"I heard the jocks say his sister found him around four thirty this morning when she got home from work," Alexandra said.

Britney smiled pertly. "I bet it's one of those ladies from the card room that killed him."

"I heard he pulled all the orchids from Edith Cohen's trees," Alex observed. "You know how much she brags about them."

"Why on earth would he do that?" Maggie asked.

"She came stomping into the bar the other day and yelled at him for being too loud. Apparently she was in the card room and his laughing was distracting her. She probably lost the hand and needed an excuse. I guess he just ignored her ranting and continued to eat his lunch, so she grabbed him by the arm to get his attention. When he stood up to face her she screamed at him to 'sit his fat ass down.' He was so shocked he actually sat down. Doc spoke up and said she should shut her mouth and go back to the card room. All the guys turned back to their business, trying to ignore her. She then said, 'Obviously none of you have ever lived in a country club.' The guys thought Marco should file a grievance but he was determined to handle it his own way."

"Isn't she the lady that was sitting at the table near us on New Year's Eve?" Maggie asked.

"Yes, remember she was the one that took the centerpiece off our table and put it on the floor because she couldn't see the countdown on the giant screen behind us?"

"That's right." Britney nodded. "I think she's crazy."

"She's also the reason for Marco's last suspension," Alex said.

"What did he do?"

"She parked her cart by the side door of the clubhouse—it's not even a parking spot but she's claimed it as her own private spot. So, as she walked past the cart barn, she heard Marco say, 'Fucking idiot!' I guess someone had backed into his cart, leaving a huge scratch. Edith went right into the manager's office and filed a grievance for his foul language."

"He does have a temper," Maggie observed. "I've heard him cuss out a few people; but I think he's a nice guy overall."

"You mean he used to be," corrected Alexandra.

"I can't believe he's dead," Britney said.

"Me either," Maggie replied.

The three women sat silently for a few moments, each remembering Marco in their own way.

"Oh my God," Maggie said suddenly. "I have a great idea."

Britney said, "What is it?"

"I am going to write a book."

"I thought you were already writing a book?" Alexandra said.

"Yeah, it's a historical fiction. I've been working on it for over ten years. I vowed to finish it when I retired…but honestly? It's just too boring. I think I should switch gears and write a murder mystery."

"I love a good mystery," Alex said.

"It will take place in Boca. I can use Marco's murder but just change all the names. We can secretly work on the case. We're three smart women…we'll probably solve it before the cops."

Maggie looked at the other two women, waiting for their response.

"I'm in," Britney said. "Sounds fun."

"I've got nothing better to do for two weeks, so why not?" Alexandra said. "We can brainstorm during happy hour."

"I'm so excited. I have so many great ideas for characters,"

Maggie told her friends.

"Ha ha ha," Britney replied. "That's not hard." She raised her arms then spread them apart, indicating everybody in the room.

Maggie had already taken her phone out. She opened the phone's notebook app and started typing. So she didn't notice the tall, suited man approach their table.

"Hello, ladies," the man greeted.

"Hello," Britney said first.

"May I?" He pointed to the empty fourth chair directly across from Maggie.

"Please," Alex said, motioning for him to sit.

"I'm Detective Mike Marker," the man said as he sat down. "I'm looking into the death of Marco Escobar."

Maggie's eyes instantly drifted from the handsome man's electric-blue eyes to the man's left hand. And there it was, a ring. Alexandra noticed Maggie's attention wavering then kicked her under the table.

"Did any of you know him?" the detective asked. He held a small flip-style notebook, a pen at the ready.

"We all know him," Britney volunteered.

"But, not that well," Maggie said quickly.

"Yeah, not that well," Alex added.

"Have any of you had interactions with him, business or social interactions?"

"We all have, we live in a country club. I mean the social part, not the business part," Maggie said, receiving another kick from Alex.

"To be honest, it wasn't an accident that I sat at this table," Detective Marker said. "A few of your 'friends' here"—he motioned around the room—"have named you three as people who may have insight into his life."

Britney looked around, shaking her head. "These people really have nothing to do."

"You know what?" the detective said, standing, "I'm going to extend an invitation downtown, at my office this afternoon, maybe around three o'clock? That way we can have some privacy. What do you say, ladies?"

"Do we need lawyers?" Britney asked.

Detective Marker raised one eyebrow. "Do you think you might need a lawyer?"

"I think we're good," Alex said. "Anything we can do to help find whoever murdered Marco."

"Did I say anything about murder?" Detective Marker asked.

"No, but word around here travels fast. It's only breakfast, imagine what the rumors will be by happy hour?" Maggie said, smiling too big.

"That's what I'm hoping for," the detective said, extending to each of them a business card he retrieved from the front pocket of his pants. "My personal cell is on the back, just in case you need it; otherwise, call the number on the front. I look forward to seeing each of you at the station this afternoon."

"Will do," Britney said.

She took all three cards from Detective Marker then handed one to each of the ladies.

"Looking forward to it," Maggie said, as the detective walked over to the teachers.

The three friends knew the teachers hadn't known Marco personally but could attest to all his transgressions. The jocks had all known him well, as that was his clique. None of the academics had known him well enough, other than to point him out.

"You weren't obvious enough," Alex said to Maggie.

"What?"

"You almost fell out of your chair," Britney said, laughing.

"You never know when the next Prince Charming will walk into your life."

"I guarantee it's not going to be behind these gates," Alexandra said. "Believe me."

"I do believe you," Maggie returned, "that's why we're doing happy hour off campus this afternoon."

"I'll get us a car," Britney said. She looked down at the detective's card in her hand. "We can have the driver deliver us downtown to the detective's office, and when we're done, we can go somewhere in West Palm since we'll already be there."

"Great idea," Maggie said. "There's that place downtown called Moscow Mule, maybe we could stop there. This," she added, "is going to be *so* much fun."

"Don't get so excited, Maggie," Alex cautioned, "this is serious stuff. Just watch what information you give this guy. You could be a suspect."

"I didn't murder anyone," Maggie replied.

"No innocent person is in prison either," Britney said sarcastically.

Maggie looked at the card in her hand. She turned it over and smiled.

CHAPTER 3

Mango Margaritas

The limo driver walked into the bar where the three women were sitting. A single glass of wine stood in front of them. They agreed that one drink wouldn't affect their interviews: it was more a liquid confidence builder.

They took the final sips of the wine then followed the driver to where he had parked the limo-style, black Sprinter van pulled in front of the club.

"Why such a big car?" Maggie asked Britney.

"It was the same price as a regular limo. So why not? If we pick up some men tonight, there's lots of room."

"Makes sense to me," Alex said.

She climbed aboard, taking the driver's hand as assistance.

The ladies sat on the limo's lowest level, a narrow table between them. Three glasses of champagne, each filled nicely, were arranged neatly on the table.

"Why not?"

Britney grabbed the glass closest to her then raised it to offer a toast. The other two women followed suit.

"To Marco, may he rest in peace," Britney said.

The three friends clinked glasses then each took a drink.

The forty-five-minute drive to the Palm Beach County

sheriff's department gave the three women time to finish off the bottle as well as discuss their characters in Maggie's book.

"I'll be Nancy Drew," Maggie said.

"I'll be Miss Marple," Alex said.

"Who should I be?" Britney asked.

"How about Veronica Mars," Maggie said.

"I think she's a teenager," Britney said.

"So is Nancy Drew. I think we're focusing on *era* not *age*. Can you think of someone else you would rather be?" Alexandra asked.

Britney stayed quiet for a minute, contemplating. "Fine, I'll be Veronica Mars. At least she's young."

"I wonder if we can record our interviews?" Maggie said.

"I'm pretty sure that would be a 'no,'" Britney replied.

"Okay, but just try as hard as you can to remember everything they say," Maggie suggested. "We should come up with a suspect list. Who do we know who would have a reason to kill Marco?

"I'm sure it's someone we don't know," Alex said.

"We're three smart ladies," Maggie observed. "I bet we could figure out who killed Marco."

"Rodney, Alan, all of the card ladies..." Britney said as Maggie typed the names into her phone.

"We're here," the driver announced from the front seat. He pulled in front of the station.

The building was more depressing than Maggie had imagined—more so as they walked through the door, where they were greeted by Detective Marker. He was now dressed in a uniform instead of the suit he had worn to the club. Maggie thought the dark green uniform made the detective even more handsome. His detective's star was pinned to one side, and an American flag was pinned on the other side. Maggie was sure his rank among the other detectives in the department must be high, because several stripes decorated his sleeve.

"You're late, ladies," Detective Marker said, looking at his watch. "But thanks for coming in."

"Not our fault," Britney said, "the traffic sucks this time of day."

The detective turned and motioned them to follow him. He opened a beat-up metal door and gestured for them to step inside.

The ladies stood frozen. They faced a solid white table in the center of the room. The table was bolted to the floor. There were four metal chairs.

"Please, take a seat," Detective Marker said.

The three women looked at each other. Shrugging, Alex pulled a chair out. She carefully inspected it before she sat down. Britney and Maggie followed suit. Detective Marker handed each of the women a clipboard and a pen.

"If you ladies could just fill in what you can on these forms, it will save us some time. I'll come back and take you one at a time for a short interview." He looked at each of the women. "Is that okay?"

The girls silently nodded.

After the detective had left, Britney looked around the room. "What do you think that is?" she said, pointing to a long brown smear on one of the walls.

"Oh my God," Maggie exclaimed, "what are we doing here?"

"I don't know...why *are* we here?" Britney echoed.

"Obviously they think Marco was murdered—and they believe we can provide some information," Alex said. As a CEO, Alex was obviously used to handling uncomfortable situations. She sat up straight, her hands folded on the table in front of her.

"Well, I doubt it was an accident," Britney said. "The guy was connected."

"What do you mean 'connected'? Like 'mob' connected?" Maggie asked.

"Seriously, Maggie? Can you be this naïve at fifty-five years old?"

"Remember, I'm from a po-dunk town in Washington State. We still believe in Bigfoot."

"It just happens that he lived in the same neighborhood as my ex-boyfriend in New York," Britney said. "I think I told you about the guy that just went to prison. He owned that cigar bar down on Military Highway."

"Why did he go to prison?" Maggie asked.

"I'm not really sure, but the other night at O'Malley's, Marco brought me a green tea shot...it was obvious it wasn't his first shot of the night. He said he knew Brandon. I pretended to not know what he was talking about. He said Brandon was a rat and he was going to get what he deserved. It freaked me out. I haven't had anything to do with Brandon since college! I knew he was doing some things a little unsavory and didn't want it to affect my business. As a matter of fact, a few years ago, the FBI came and asked me some questions, but I didn't know anything."

"Wow, Britney." Alex shook her head in disbelief. "I can't believe you never told us about this."

"I have no idea how Marco knew I had anything to do with Brandon," Britney insisted. "I don't want to get mixed up with these guys. I called my dad, he knows people. He made some calls and said I was safe."

"Your dad knows Mafia people?"

"I never said Mafia."

"You didn't have to," Maggie said.

"I was seeing him," Alex said all of a sudden.

"Who?" the other two said in unison.

"Marco." Alex shook her head.

"*What?*" Maggie tried to imagine this sophisticated older woman actually on a date with Marco. "How?"

"*Why?*" Britney wanted to know, narrowing her eyes.

"He was a good-looking guy," Alex explained simply. She obviously wanted to defend herself, although she knew she didn't have to. "We just happened to be the only two people at the bar for lunch one day. We started discussing business and ended up discussing our favorite Italian restaurants. We decided to try out. We even golfed a couple of times."

"How long had you been seeing him?" Maggie asked.

Alex shrugged. "A year."

"*A year?*" Maggie and Britney asked in unison.

Alex leaned back with a Cheshire Cat smile.

"How did we not know about this?" Britney asked.

"I can't believe you never said anything," Maggie added. She smiled, forgetting the guy was now dead.

"I thought he had a wife?" Britney said.

"The woman that lives with him is his sister," Alex said. "Her name is Angie, she's going through a divorce. Apparently, her ex is a big asshole and was stalking her—so she moved in with Marco."

"Did you sleep with him?" Maggie asked.

Alex sat back in her chair with an overexaggerated shocked look on her face but her tight lips soon melted into a smile.

"A lady never tells," Alex said, exposing a New York accent that she usually had under control. They all broke out into laughter.

"They say Latin lovers are the best," Maggie said.

"He's Italian," Alex said.

"I thought he was from Argentina...or Brazil...or some country like that," Britney said.

"He was actually born in Brazil. His parents were some kind of diplomats. But he's *definitely* Italian," Alex said.

Maggie raised her left eyebrow. "I guess you would know."

Just then the door burst open. The tall detective moved into the room, shutting them into a dead silence. He looked at each of them for a moment with his piercing blue eyes, as though he were trying to decide which of them looked the most guilty. Or maybe he was merely contemplating which of them he would take first for an interview? His gaze finally settled on Maggie, who seemed to be nearly jumping out of her chair to go first.

The detective must have noticed her excited state. He pointed his index finger at her, curling it, motioning for her to follow him. Maggie stood and headed out the door, pausing for a moment before turning around and giving the other two ladies a small wave. She flashed a huge smile. Alex shook her head but gave her a small wave in return. Brittany gave her a double thumbs-up.

As Maggie followed the detective, she couldn't help looking at his left hand, saddened to see the detective's ring was still there. She smiled to herself, shaking her head. Even if this guy wasn't married, he definitely would have a girlfriend. One thing she had realized at fifty-five years old, if a handsome guy with a real job wasn't attached in some way, there was definitely something wrong with him. That was the reason Maggie had stopped internet dating. The last handsome man she had met online and had actually started dating lived with his mother...*and* her twenty cats. When he told her he didn't have a job because he was taking care of his mother, she was impressed—until, that is, she found out his mother was actually supporting him because he didn't have a job.

They finally reached the door at the end of a hallway that seemed to never end. The detective opened the door and motioned Maggie in. As she entered, she got a whiff of the clean scent of Detective Marker's aftershave. It made her knees buckle a bit.

The room was the size of a janitor's closet. It had been transformed into an office: an old wooden desk piled with files sat in the center. Detective Mike Marker took a seat in the desk chair. It had a worn green cushion that didn't look comfortable.

Maggie sat down in a chair that looked like an old dining room chair; it did not have any padding. "They ran out of real offices and put you in a broom closet?"

"How's your day so far?" the detective asked, ignoring Maggie's comment. He shifted a pile of loose files, moving it atop another pile to clear a spot in front of him. He took a yellow legal pad out of a side drawer and moved his glasses from the bridge of his nose closer to his light blue eyes. He had dark grey hair cut short on the sides, possibly to hide the fact he was completely bald on top.

"Name?"

"Maggie."

He looked at her sideways "Full name."

"Oh, of course. Margret Anne McFarlin.

"Can you spell each name?"

Instead of answering him, she dug through her purse and handed him her driver's license. He looked over his glasses but didn't object. He probably knew it was a good idea.

He gestured to the license. "Is this your correct address?"

"Yes, it is," Maggie said.

"So how did you know Mr. Escobar?"

"He was a member of our club."

"How long had you known him and when was the last time you saw him."

"He came to my house over a year ago, when I first moved here. He picked up some old furniture. And then I saw him a few times at O'Malley's. We had a few conversations here and there. He seemed like a nice guy, just a little rough around the edges."

"Who were his friends?"

"I only know the people at the club…but I'm not sure if they were his actual friends."

"Would you know of anyone at the club who might have a problem with him?"

"No," Maggie said, but in her head she had a two-page list.

"Have you ever seen him get into an argument or disagreement with anyone."

"I've heard second-hand accounts of disagreements with some of the people at the club," she said.

"Have you actually witnessed any of these disagreements?"

"Yeah, one."

"Can you tell me about it?" Detective Marker asked. He positioned his pen over his legal pad. "Try not to leave anything out, I want to hear even the most insignificant detail."

"It was probably a month after I moved here, and I didn't

really know anyone yet," Maggie began. "I went to the club bar for lunch. Marco was sitting in his normal spot with his back against the wall, facing the door, and Mr. Byron, not sure of his first name but he's a long-time member, sat at the opposite end of the bar with another man I didn't recognize. Marco's cell phone rang and he answered it. He wasn't really talking, mostly listening, but it bothered Mr. Byron. He actually got up out of his chair and stood right behind Marco then tells him to get off the phone. Marco just waves him off. Mr. Byron didn't move but started raising his voice, telling Marco to get off the phone. Marco just took the phone away from his ear and said, 'What the hell is wrong with you?' That's when Fonzie, the bartender, saw the trouble and came over to the two men."

Maggie paused, shifting in the chair. Then she continued: "Mr. Byron starts yelling at Fonzie, 'It's your job to enforce club rules at the bar. You're not allowed to be on your cell phone when you're sitting at the bar, so tell him to get off the phone.' Marco finally pulled the phone away from his ear and stood up to face Mr. Byron. He said, 'I don't know what your problem is, pal, but you need to get out of my face and out of my business.' Then Mr. Byron said something like, 'Your kind don't belong here. I've been a member for thirteen years and I've seen your kind come and go. It won't be long, you'll be gone.' Then Marco laughed and said, 'Over my dead body.'"

Detective Marker wrote down notes as Maggie spoke but didn't react.

"What was the bartender's name again?"

"Fonzie," Maggie said.

"Fonzie?"

"Yeah, that's what we call him. I don't think that's his real name but that's what everyone calls him," Maggie told the detective again. "I think it's because of his hair. You know, kind of greased back and combed up, like Fonzie from that show *Happy Days*."

"Okay, Fonzie." Detective Marker wrote a few more notes as Maggie stayed silent. "Did you know the other person sitting with Mr. Byron?"

"No. I don't remember seeing him again, but I was distracted by the whole confrontation."

The detective riffled through one of the piles of folders. From somewhere in the middle of the pile he brought out the club directory and handed it to Maggie. "Look through that and see if you recognize him."

Maggie flipped through the pages, looking at each of the members' photograph. She did not see the other guy who had been in the bar.

"No luck?" the detective asked.

She shook her head. "Nope, sorry."

"If you think of anything else, even a small thing, please give me a call. My cell number is on the back of the card I gave you this morning."

"Yep, got it."

Maggie nodded then stood up, ready to go. Detective Marker opened the door and let her walk ahead until she reached the room where the other two were sitting. Then she took a deep breath.

"Next," Detective Marker said. He motioned to Alex, who stood and followed him back to his so-called office. Fewer than ten minutes later, Alex came back and sat down. Britney was led back.

"Well, that was fast," Maggie said.

"I asked for a lawyer."

"Why?"

"Because I can," she said confidently.

"Did he ask you about dating Marco?"

"Shhh. No," Alex said, looking around. "I just wasn't in the mood to answer any questions. I learned a long time ago, never give information too freely."

"Probably a smart idea." Maggie nodded. "Good thing I don't know anything."

"You were gone a long time for not knowing anything," Alex said.

"I told him about that guy that got in a fight over a phone call. He'll probably ask Fonzie about it," Maggie said.

"Why Fonzie?"

"He was there."

"Fonzie probably hears a lot behind that bar; but I guarantee he won't remember a thing." Alex smiled with confidence, having let her accent free again.

Finally, Britney came bouncing down the hall.

"Let's go," she said, heading for the door.

"Ladies." Detective Marker had followed them to the front steps. "I'll let you know if I have any further questions. Don't leave town."

Maggie turned back to look at him. "Seriously?"

"No, you can leave town"—he smiled—"but I'll be in contact."

He watched the driver open the door and help all three women into the black Sprinter that had been waiting nearby. He shook his head as they ducked behind the dark tinted glass.

*

"Where to, ladies?" the driver behind the wheel of the Sprinter called back to the three women.

"Let's go back to Boca and stop at Casa Tequila instead of Moscow Mules," Britney suggested.

"Sounds good to me," Alex said. "Close to home."

When they entered Casa Tequila, they saw all the seats at one end of the bar were open. Fortunately. Then again, it was early. They took their seats, Britney already busy texting on her phone. She had been busy texting ever since leaving the police station.

"You okay?" Maggie asked.

"Yeah, yeah," Britney said. "That was just crazy. I need a drink!"

"That was intense," Maggie agreed.

"Seriously?" Alex looked over the menu she held calmly in front of her face. "It was nothing. I don't know why he brought us down there at all. A total waste of time."

"I thought it was sort of fun," Maggie replied. "I've never been interviewed. Especially by such a hunky cop."

"You *really* need a date," Britney said.

"As a matter of fact, I do," Maggie said.

"Me too," Alex said.

"What are you ladies having today?" the bartender asked from across the bar.

"Three mango margaritas, please," Alex told the bartender.

Britney finally put her phone down but was still obviously distracted.

"Everything okay?" Maggie asked again.

"Of course." Britney shrugged. "Just needed to text my dad."

When the drinks arrived the orangey concoction in each of the three glasses threatened to spill over. The bartender had filled them so close to the brim each of the three ladies had to lean over to sip directly from her oversized glass. It was a few minutes before they could safely pick up the glasses to make a toast.

CHAPTER 4

Mimosas

The first round of golfers was heading out from the starter booth in front of the Water's Edge course. Of the two courses the club offered residents, the three women preferred the Tree Line course: Britney used Louis Vuitton golf balls, which were not cheap. The retrieval rate for balls that went astray was higher in the woods than from the water.

The three women had gathered at the driving range. Alexandra sported dark sunglasses that covered half her face; she had probably chosen them as a result of the many margaritas she had consumed the previous evening. Maggie wore her hair pulled back; it was covered with a hat. She hadn't even bothered putting makeup on. Then there was Britney. She looked like she had just walked out of the pages of *Golf Digest*. She wore a sleeveless baby blue golf shirt, a matching skirt, and white knee socks. Her hair hung in long thick braids on either side of her head.

"How can she look so refreshed?" Maggie asked Alex.

"Youth," Alex said.

Britney laughed at the women. They were obviously suffering. "I have a remedy for what ails you," she said. She smiled and walked to the back of her golf cart.

Britney's golf cart was amazing. That was the only word for it. Even while remaining faithful to all the club restrictions, she had utilized her creative talents to modify the club car into something straight out of a James Bond film. It was a bright winter white, like all the other carts in the club, but she had added special large tires with flat black aluminum wheels that probably cost more than the cart itself. She had bright blue faux-ostrich-skin covered seats with a matching rain guard fashioned after the furnishings in the hotel lobby she had recently designed in Dubai. But the ultimate modification was located directly behind the passenger seat where she had installed a refrigerated bar stocked with a variety of mini bottles. The bar was circular in design, and it took up most of the space in the back. There was just enough room behind the driver's seat for her clubs.

She pushed a lever, releasing the top section of the bar and exposing a bucket of ice with a nice bottle of champagne and plenty of orange juice for their Saturday morning golf game. She pulled out the bottle and removed the screen around the top before wrapping her golf towel around the entire neck of the bottle, releasing the cork with a muffled *pop!*

"Mimosas," she said, smiling wide. She poured three glasses until they were almost filled with the prosecco and a top off of orange juice—just enough for color.

Alexandra held up her thick plastic champagne flute. "Cheers."

"Cheers," the other two said in unison, tapping all three glasses together.

They heard the starter call on the club's intercom just as they finished their first glass, and they headed across to the course.

The first hole was miserable for Maggie and Britney. As usual. Maggie completely missed the ball on her first try teeing off, and Britney topped her tee shot, sending her ball maybe fifty yards down the fairway. However, Alexandra was her normal consistent self: she smacked that small white ball perfectly straight, approximately one hundred yards, using her 1-wood.

The three ladies climbed into their golf carts and rode

down to their balls. First up: Britney. She hit her ball. It again maybe traveled another fifty yards.

"Slow down, girls," Alex said. "Sing 'Moon River.'"

"'Moon River'?" Britney said.

"*Moon* on the back swing," she said, demonstrating without a ball in front of her. "*River* as you swing forward."

Maggie took a 5-hybrid out of her bag and lined up in front of her ball.

"*Mooooon…riiiiiver…*" she sang as she swung the club. But she completely missed the ball.

"Keep your eye on the ball," Alex said.

"I might need some more aiming fluid."

Maggie retrieved her empty glass from her cart then ambled over to the back of Britney's cart for a refill.

By the third hole the alcohol had the desired effect. Maggie and Britney started to hit the ball as they sang *moon river* with each swing. They had improved their game enough to achieve forward momentum. Meanwhile Alex continued to be on task.

"Let's just do nine," Maggie said. "It's so muggy, and it's going to rain." She turned her red face to the dark clouds looming in the distance.

"I agree," Alex said.

Britney handed her a refill.

The next hole was the best hole they played, but the skies continued to turn dark. The air was thick with moisture. Just when they were about to tee off on Number 5 the lighting siren sang loudly, warning all the golfers to seek shelter. Maggie secretly thanked the heavens for the electrified skies as they all agreed the clubhouse bar was the nearest shelter.

With all three golf carts lined up, they headed down the cart path, when Britney stopped suddenly. Alex came up on one side and Maggie drove up on the other.

"Wait a second," Britney said, pointing across the course.

"What?" Maggie asked.

"It's Marco's house." She still was pointing at the light

brown villa house, the yellow police tape still draped around the back fence. "Let's go check it out."

"I don't think that's a good idea," Maggie said.

"If anyone says anything we can just say we were taking a shortcut because of the lightning."

"I'm in," Alex said.

"Fine, I'll go—but we are *not* going in," Maggie said.

"Park between his house and the one on the left," Alexandra instructed, pointing to the space between the two houses. "Those people are snowbirds and won't be back until November."

Britney led the pack and pulled up as close as she could, utilizing the large bougainvillea bushes as a barrier to avoid being in full view of the street. Alex pulled in directly behind her, and Maggie came third in line.

"We'll just look through the windows—but don't touch anything," Maggie said, "we don't want our fingerprints found at a crime scene."

Britney led the girls through the back gate. The sky had gone almost completely black, and thunder rumbled in the background. All three women drew their faces close to the glass sliding doors, trying to see inside, but the lights were out, and the darkness behind them hid any object that was even close.

"I can see the blood," Britney said.

"Where?" Alex asked, moving closer to Britney.

"Right there." Britney pointed to a dark spot on the tile.

"I can't believe they haven't cleaned it up," Maggie said.

"They never do," Alex said. "It's up to the homeowner."

"How would you know that?" Britney asked her.

"A friend of mine was accidentally shot in the head. He was screwing around with his gun, pretending to shoot himself. He didn't realize there was a bullet in the chamber. He actually shot himself in the head. Brain and bone blew all over the room. My friend and her sister had to clean it up. She was picking up small chards of bone for months."

Britney stared at Alex. "Why didn't she hire someone to

clean it up?"

"I don't think she could afford it. That was the days we were young and poor."

"You were poor?" Maggie asked Alex.

"And young." She smiled.

Britney used her golf towel and tried the door, but it was locked. The house was the exact same layout as her own, so she knew the side slider was the entrance to Marco's bedroom. She decided to try it…and fortunately it was not locked.

"Hey," she whispered loudly, "this door is unlocked!"

"We are *definitely* not going in there," Alex said.

"Oh, hell yeah, we are," Britney said. She disappeared into the dark house.

"Just don't touch anything," Maggie called. She looked around, hoping none of the neighbors was paying attention.

A flash of lightning followed by a loud crash of thunder made them all jump.

"I wonder if Marco's ghost lives here?" Britney asked.

"His house is a mess," Maggie said. "He must not have had a housekeeper."

Britney found the kitchen light and switched it on. Maggie looked cautiously around the room and recognized the coffee table that used to be in her house. It was a large square glass table supported by four granite posts. She had bought her house fully furnished, and the style of the previous owners' furniture didn't match hers; so she had given away most everything that was originally there. Marco was a godsend: he agreed to take everything, and he even sent a crew to pick it all up. She had even tried to tip them, but they wouldn't accept one dime.

Maggie was careful not to touch anything as she walked through the kitchen. She watched as Britney thumbed through what looked like a pile of mail on Marco's desk. She was just about to remind Britney not to touch anything when she noticed a bottle of wine with two glasses sitting near the sink.

"It looked like Marco was expecting company," she said aloud, but the other two were busy looking around and didn't respond.

Maggie used the golf towel she still had in her hand to turn the wine so she could see the label. A 2016 Château Mouton Rothschild wine. Two glasses. It was a very expensive bottle of wine…so it must have been a very special person. Maggie might drink house wine, but she did know about wine. That particular bottle was not to share with Rodney. Marco must have been expecting a more important guest. Rodney wouldn't know a Château Mouton from a Manischewitz.

"You finding anything in there?" Alexandra was still standing near the door.

"It looks like he was past due on all of his bills," Britney said. Maggie noticed Britney looking through a small notebook but didn't notice her putting it back as she continued to riffle through the papers. "Here's his club statement," she said as she ripped it open.

"What are you doing?" Maggie asked.

"Oh my." Britney held the statement as if they all could read it in the dark room.

"What?" Alexandra said, taking a few steps toward Britney.

The three women were leaning in to look at the statement when the front door flew open. They jumped back, and Britney dropped the statement.

"Hands up!" a loud voice yelled.

Detective Marker and a young deputy advanced slowly, their guns drawn, pointed at the three women. "What the hell are you doing in here?" Detective Marker asked.

"Don't shoot." Britney kept her arms high in the air. "It's just us girls."

"We're not going to shoot you…but we should arrest you," Detective Marker said as he slowly holstered his weapon. The deputy behind him followed his supervisor's lead. He was young, and his gaze was solely focused on Britney.

"What did we do?" Britney asked. Noting the deputy's gaze, she batted her huge brown eyes for effect.

"Breaking and entering is a good start, or how about contaminating a crime scene?"

Detective Marker leaned down and picked up the statement that Britney had dropped. He looked at it then handed it back to the deputy, who put it in a plastic bag then wrote on it with a Sharpie he retrieved from his pocket.

Maggie spoke up in their defense. "We were just curious."

"I guess you never heard of the cat?"

"Guess not," Britney said and then whispered to Alex: "The cat?"

"Britney!" Alex said softly. "Stop."

"You better listen to your friend over there," Detective Marker said, jerking his head toward Alex. "You ladies are in a lot of trouble. I should be arresting all three of you, but honestly, the paperwork isn't worth it, because I don't actually believe you had anything to do with this…but I *am* going to warn you. If I catch even the slightest hint that you are near this house again I will arrest you, no question. As a matter of fact, I'll do it on a Friday night after all the judges go home so you'll be locked up until Monday morning. I'm sure they don't have happy hour in the county jail."

The girls didn't say a thing. Instead, they followed him out the front door as the deputy stayed behind to lock the back slider. He checked every other window and door as well to make sure everything was secure.

"We are really sorry, Detective," Maggie said.

"You should be," he said. "Now, stay out of trouble."

They all nodded then climbed into their golf carts. When they were safely around the corner, out of the detective's sight, they pulled up next to each other.

"That was intense," Maggie said.

"I'm just glad he didn't arrest us," Alex replied.

"Come on, ladies, haven't you heard of night court?" Britney said. "We would be out before midnight." She laughed then took off at high speed. There was no way their carts could catch up with hers; so Alex and Maggie drove side by side, toward the clubhouse bar; but the rain increased in intensity. Soon it was falling too heavily for the two ladies to continue. So they decided to park their carts in the nearest shelter, which happened to be the cart barn. They drove under cover just as the parking lot became a lake.

"You just made it," José said as he handed the two women several towels to dry themselves with. He used a few extra towels to wipe down their carts.

Alex dried her face with the towel José had just given her. "You don't mind if we wait it out here, do you?"

"Of course you can," José said.

"I wonder where Britney went?" Alex asked Maggie.

Maggie pulled out her phone from her back pocket and texted Britney.

> Maggie: *Where are you?*
> Britney: *Rodney's*
> Maggie: *Why?*
> Britney: *His garage was open when the rain came.*
> Maggie: *So, what are you doing now?*
> Britney: *Drinking wine.*
> Maggie: *Since you're there, find out everything you can about what happened at Marco's.*
> Britney: *I'm on it.*

"Where is she?" Alexandra asked.

"Rodney's."

"Why?" Alexandra said, scrunching up her nose.

"First open garage."

Alex shrugged. "I guess that makes sense."

José was still busy toweling off the golf carts and releasing the rain guards so Alex and Maggie could drive off when the rain let up.

"Did you hear about Marco?" Maggie asked José.

"Oh, yes," José said. He stopped his activity to face the two women. "Very sad....He was a very nice guy and always a good tipper."

"He was a great guy," Alex said, letting José know they were all on the same side.

José finished zipping the last section on Alexandra's cart when he pointed to a cart in the corner. "I'm not sure what we should do with his cart," he said.

"That's his cart?" Maggie's interest was piqued.

José nodded. "We installed new tires last week but now I don't know what to do."

Maggie looked out at the rain, which showed no sign of slowing down.

"Do you have any coffee?"

"No," José said, "but I can make some."

"That would be great," Maggie said, "if you wouldn't mind…"

"I think we're stuck here for a while," Alex said.

"I'll be back in a few minutes."

Jose disappeared into his office. As soon as they figured he was busy, both women quietly went over to Marco's golf cart. The front storage compartment was full of typical golfer's gear: a cigar clipper, glove, sunglasses, a few random tees and some well-used balls that looked like he fished out of the lake's edge.

"Look in his bag," Maggie whispered.

Alexandra unzipped and rezipped pockets until she slipped her hand into the long pocket on the side. She pulled out a piece of paper just as José stepped out of the office holding two cups of coffee. Maggie stood in front of Alexandra as she put the folded paper into her pocket.

"These are nice tires," Alexandra said. "Do you think it's time for mine to be replaced?"

José looked over at Alex's cart. "No," he said handing the two women their cups, "you have lots of time."

"Okay, good," she said "But I want bigger wheels next time."

"You're a cool lady," José said, smiling.

The two women sat on the wooden bench, the only seating available in the cart barn, and silently drank their coffee. Both were so eager to look at the paper Alexandra had found, hoping it was a valuable clue. But José kept a pretty close eye on the two as he kept himself busy moving carts around, organizing shelves, and sweeping the floor. There was no opportunity to pull the paper out without him noticing.

"More coffee?" he asked.

"No, thank you," Maggie said.

"Would you mind if we leave our carts here and go to the locker room?" Alexandra asked.

"Not at all," Jose said. "If the rain stops, I will pull them around."

"Perfect," Maggie said.

Holding towels over their heads, the two women ran the short distance from the cart barn to the ladies' locker room. They looked down the banks of lockers, making sure they were alone, then sat on the bench in the center. Alexandra pulled the paper from her pocket, unfolded it, and set it on the bench between them.

"It's an address," Alexandra said.

Maggie pulled her phone from her pocket and typed the address into Google. She scrolled down a few screens. "This is weird," she said.

"What is it?"

"It's that hotel project deal that Britney's friend went to jail for."

"Really?"

Alexandra left the bench to stand behind Maggie and better see what she was seeing.

"There's a whole article here saying some of the investors who were ripped off were from Brazil."

"Oh," Alex said, "shit."

Maggie stopped reading and looked at Alex.

"What?"

"Nothing."

Alex stepped back, obviously deep in thought, and obviously bothered with the finding.

"You know something about this, don't you, Alex?"

Alex remained silent. Maggie couldn't read her. She decided not to push it.

"Let's go get a drink," Maggie suggested.

"Good idea. But I need to run home for a minute. I'll be right behind you."

Maggie didn't have an opportunity to respond. Alex had already turned back toward the rear door.

CHAPTER 5

House Cabernet

The club bar was unusually quiet for this time in the afternoon. The summer weather often had that effect on the full-time residents who chose to stay home rather than face the torrential rain. The sounds of '70s rock welcomed Maggie as she entered the side door, looking a bit frazzled but ready for a drink. The music was an improvement from the elevator music that used to play throughout the clubhouse when Maggie had first joined the club.

Maggie took her usual seat at the end of the bar. "Where are the guys?" she asked Fonzie.

Fonzie wiped a wine glass before he set the glass in front of her then filled it with the house Cabernet.

"They're in the locker room playing cards," he said.

"The locker room?"

"Apparently the gentlemen in the men's card room complained that 'our guys' were too loud. So the party moved into the locker room."

Maggie stared hard at Fonzie. "Seriously?"

"They removed a bank of lockers, moved some benches and set up a table; they even installed a phone so they can just call when they need a drink." He pointed to the wall phone behind the bar.

"I'm surprised the board approved that," Maggie said.

"Well, that's a whole other issue," Fonzie said, rolling his eyes.

"What's an issue?" Alex asked. She sat down on the bar stool next to Maggie.

Maggie pointed to the empty round table in the corner. "The guys," she said.

Fonzie silently placed a glass in front of Alex. "Cabernet?"

Alex smiled to him. "No, I think I'll have a sauvignon blanc."

Fonzie quickly moved the wider wine glass aside and replaced it with a white wine glass. He pulled the bottle from the cooler below the bar and poured a generous glass.

"Thank you, sweetie," Alex said. She lifted her glass to Maggie. "Cheers."

"Cheers." They each took a sip from their glass. "That was a quick trip home."

"I changed my mind," Alex said with the same unreadable face.

"I am *so* confused," Maggie said.

"Where's Britney?" Alex asked, changing the subject.

"I just got a text. She had an appointment on the island," Maggie said. "She'll be here soon."

"I wonder if it's the Breakers Hotel? I love the Breakers," Alex said.

"Who doesn't?"

"So where are the guys?" Alex pointed to the table in the corner.

"You're not going to believe this. They're in the men's locker room, playing cards."

Maggie scoffed. "What? Why?"

"The old fuddy-duddies in the card room complained that they were too loud, so they modified the men's locker room, turning it into a private card area just for the guys."

"Of course they did. Lord help us if we have a little fun around this place."

Maggie smiled. "No fun allowed."

Alex nodded then took a sip of her sauvignon blanc. Then she set the glass down and turned to Fonzie. "Can I get a chicken salad for lunch?"

"Of course," the bartender said. "Anything else?" He walked over to the computer and touched the screen a few times, shaking his head.

"Nope, that's it."

"Lunch?" he asked Maggie.

"No thanks, Fonz. I'm trying to lose a few pounds."

As the two women continued chatting, the wall phone rang. Fonzie picked it up before the second ring. He made a few notes in a small notebook.

Maggie's phone chimed, indicating a text. She picked it up to check the message. "Britney's here," she said.

Fonzie was busy making a tray full of drinks he had set on the bar just as Britney walked in through the dining room. She kissed Maggie on each cheek. Then she kissed Alexandra on each cheek too. Finally she sat on the stool on the other side of Maggie.

"What's up, ladies?"

"Not much," Alex said. "I can't stay too long. Nail appointment."

Britney held up her hand, showing off her Tiffany-blue fingernails. "I need to make one." The next moment she noticed Fonzie coming out from behind the bar with a tray of drinks.

"Where you going with those drinks?" Britney asked, looking around.

"The men's locker room," Fonzie said.

"The men's locker room?"

"The guys got kicked out of the card room for being loud." Maggie explained.

"You have got to be kidding."

Both Maggie and Alex shook their heads.

Britney set her purse on top of the bar, but instead of remaining in her seat she stood and followed Fonzie.

"Let me help you with the door," she said, smiling wide.

Watching Britney from the bar, Maggie and Alexandra just looked at each other.

A few minutes later, Fonzie and Britney came back, chatting.

"Oh, you girls are not going to believe this…"

"What?" they said, again in unison.

"They have a whole set up in there," Britney said. "It's great."

"You went in the men's locker room?" Maggie asked.

Britney shrugged. "Who was going to stop me?"

"That's true," Maggie said "But they're usually in here eating lunch by now."

"They got a late start. They had to wait for the rained-out golfers to clear out," she said.

Maggie shook her head. "That's crazy," she said.

"That isn't anything. Try taking a cookie out of the women's card room," Alex said.

They all laughed.

"I have an idea," Maggie said.

"Bring it," Britney replied.

"Let's finish the list of suspects we started in the limo the other day." Maggie pulled out her phone, swiping until she came to the list. "I only have Rodney and Alan," she said.

Britney dug around in her new oversized Louis Vuitton and pulled out a small notebook. "We need to do an Agatha Christie and get all the suspects in the same room."

"How are we going to do that?" Alex asked.

"A dinner party," Maggie said.

Both Maggie and Britney looked at Alex with wide smiles.

"You know we don't cook," Britney said.

"You do have the biggest house," Maggie replied.

"Come on, Alex…" Britney said. "We'll pitch in."

"You don't have to convince me." Alex winked at her friends. "I'm the hostess with the mostess."

"So…who's coming to dinner?"

"So, we have Rodney, of course," Britney said. "I mean he was there when it happened. Maybe he was so drunk he thought he was aiming at the tree and instead he hit Marco."

"You would have to be pretty drunk to shoot a guy and then fall asleep," Alex observed.

"Who else?" Maggie asked.

"Doc," Britney said.

"Why Doc?"

"There's definitely something going on between them. I was at O'Malley's last week and they were sitting at opposite sides of the bar and never even acknowledged each other."

"I actually thought they were good friends," Maggie said.

"*Friends* is a good word for it," Britney acknowledged. "… Or you could describe it more like a drug dealer–customer kind of relationship."

"I thought Doc wasn't dealing anymore?" Alexandra said.

"Maybe he owes him money or something; but whenever they're in the same room, they avoid each other like the plague," Britney said.

"Okay, definitely add him. Who else?" Maggie asked.

"How about his sister, Angie?" Britney said. "She did find the body."

"Probably an unlikely suspect," Maggie noted, "but you know what they say: usually murders are committed by someone close to the victim."

Alex shook her head. "I doubt she would show, her brother just died."

"Yeah," Maggie agreed. "But did you know she moved in with Wendy, Marco's ex-girlfriend?"

"That's weird. I didn't even know they knew each other," Britney said.

Alexandra smiled. "Let's add Wendy to the list."

"Definitely. She's a good one.' " Britney wrote it down.

"There has to be more to that story than we know," Maggie noted.

"Do you think he really sexually harassed her?"

"Of course…I believe it," Alex said. "Marco thinks he's God's gift to women. He would never take no for an answer."

"*Thought*…" Maggie said. "Past tense."

"Wendy was my favorite golf pro," Maggie said, "I was sad when she left. We actually became friends and hung out."

"She was my favorite too," Britney said. "Can you think of anyone else?"

"That's it," Maggie said.

"We need at least one more. The table seats eight, it won't look right if we have an empty chair," Alex noted.

Maggie thought for a moment. "Who else would be a good suspect?"

They sat quietly for a few minutes.

"Alan?" Britney asked. "The president of the board?"

"Definitely, he is one of our suspects." Maggie nodded to Alex. "Write him down."

"This is going to be *so* good," Britney said.

Alex turned to more practical matters. "Eight people is a lot…who can we get to help out?"

"I can ask my housekeeper," Maggie suggested. "She does this kind of thing sometimes."

"Fonzie," Alex called out, "do you know anyone who would be willing to work a party? Basically, they would just help serve food, pour drinks, and get the dishes in the dishwasher."

Fonzie raised his hand as though answering a question in grade school. "I'll do it," he said.

"Really? That would be great," she said, "are you available next Friday?"

"I'll be there." He nodded.

Just then the guys came through the locker room door, carrying their empty glasses. Fonzie immediately started lining up glasses, preparing fresh drinks.

"Ladies."

Each of the six men repeated the one-word salutation as they walked past Alex, Maggie, and Britney, kissing each of the three women on their cheeks before sitting at the large round table near the window—their regular spot for holding court.

"Who's the big winner today?" Maggie asked.

"Lenny took all our money today," Doc replied.

Alex looked at Doc unsurely. "I didn't know Lenny even played cards with you guys."

"I don't," Lenny said. "Obviously it's beginner's luck."

"Hey, Britney," Doc now asked, "do you know a guy named Brandon?"

"Brandon is a common name for guys my age," Britney said. "I must know a dozen guys named Brandon." She moved her pocketbook in front of her, making room next to her.

"I went to school with his father," Doc explained. "We had lunch the other day and he said that you dated his son."

"Huh," Britney said, "don't recall a Brandon…"

"He's in jail," Doc said.

"Really, what did he do?"

"He was involved in some financial scam involving selling green cards to foreign investors."

"It's called an EB-5 investment," Lenny spoke up. "A person can invest at least a half a million in a capital project at a company he doesn't work for and get a fast-tracked visa."

"It's that new hotel," Doc explained. "I guess he was collecting the money from investors, but instead of spending it on the project, he was spending it on himself. He bought a million-dollar home, a Ferrari, and whatever else."

"I think it might be the Brandon who owns the cigar bar down the street," Britney said.

Doc nodded. "That's him," he said.

"You know Marco hung out at that cigar bar…I wonder if there is any connection?" Alex asked.

Lenny laughed. "Who knew boring Boca could be this interesting?"

Maggie leaned over to Britney and whispered softly: "That's the guy you were telling us about."

"Yeah," Britney whispered back.

"We should go talk to him in jail..."

"Oh, hell no," Britney replied, still whispering. "I need to shake that connection as soon as possible."

"Do you know more about this than you're saying?"

"I can't talk about it. I honestly thought it all went away... Let's talk about it later."

"Darn it!" Maggie replied. "I've never visited anyone behind bars before."

"Hopefully, they'll find whoever killed Marco so everything can get back to normal!" Alex said.

"I hope there's a connection," Maggie said.

Britney raised an eyebrow. "Why are you so excited about all this?"

"My book, of course. This is motivating me to write. I have a million ideas in my head. I need to get it all on paper."

"You should talk to Larry, he was a New York City detective," Alex said.

"Really?"

Alex nodded. "I heard he actually dated Wendy after she left the club."

Maggie looked at the overly tanned white-haired man sitting at the table. Larry was not a small guy: he took up most of the space at his section of table. Maggie had heard that he played football for Florida State before he had joined the NYPD. He was single, and he could have been an option for Maggie; but as soon as she saw his "type" of girl, she settled for friendship. She was too old and much too thick.

"How are we going to contact Wendy?" Britney asked.

"I got this," Maggie said.

As soon as Larry went to the restroom, Maggie waited a minute before excusing herself to go to the ladies' room. She took her time looking at the art hanging on the walls just outside the restrooms when Larry came out.

"Hey, Larry," Maggie said.

"Hey, Maggs, what's up?"

"Not much, my golf game sucks, but otherwise life is

good."

Larry nodded his head in agreement. "Golf is one of those games you play for fun. If you take it too seriously, you'll just be frustrated."

"I need to take a few lessons," Maggie said. "I sure wish Wendy was still here. She was so much better than the guys."

"She was good," Larry said. "I have her number if you want to give her a call." He pulled his phone from his pocket.

"That would be great," Maggie said.

"Here you go." Larry forwarded the contact.

Maggie replied, "Thanks, I'll text her now. But I sure wish she were still here."

Larry smiled. "Well, maybe she can come back now."

"Why?"

"The asshole is dead. I don't know what he did, but it's his fault she's gone."

Maggie looked curiously at Larry. She considered asking another question but decided against it. "Well, thanks again for the number." She turned and walked into the ladies' room. She texted a short message to Wendy then waited a few minutes by the sink before heading out.

CHAPTER 6

Shot of Tequila

The next day, Maggie met Wendy at Southern Hills, a favorite public golf course in Boca where Wendy was able to give private lessons. It was one of those days that even in the summer made Boca feel like paradise. It was still hot but the breeze made the morning air feel tolerable.

"Thank you for doing this," Maggie said. "You're so much better than those pros at the club. You were one of the few people I could talk to when I moved to Boca."

"We have had some good talks," Wendy acknowledged.

"Mostly me telling you my problems." Maggie laughed. "You're like a hair stylist with a five-iron instead of a curling iron."

"How are you doing with that five-iron?" Wendy asked.

"Much better considering I never even took the cover off of it before I took lessons with you." She laughed again. "We need to get together more, both professionally and just for fun."

"Sounds great. I'm only working three days a week now so I have plenty of time."

"Only three days?"

"I'm going back to school to get my personal trainer certificate."

Wendy pulled a few clubs from Maggie's bag. Maggie felt

like a giant standing next to her; the golf pro was a petite five foot two. Wendy was also at least fifteen years younger—and in a lot better shape than Maggie.

"That's cool," Maggie said. "I'll hire you."

When she had first moved to Florida, Maggie attempted to fight her age. She had tried to get in good enough shape to look like she was forty again; but fighting the slow decline of her body—as most women in Boca did—had proved too exhausting. Maybe having Wendy as her trainer would allow her to get motivated again.

"It's something I've always wanted to do but never had the means," Wendy said. "Funny how things work out sometimes."

"Yeah, funny."

Maggie could not let go that Wendy was somehow financing her school.

For the next half hour Wendy straightened out Maggie's stance and pushed her elbow up and encouraged her to follow through. She even recorded Maggie's swing using an iPad. Then she played back the video to show Maggie where she was lacking. By the end of the session, Maggie was making full contact with her driver almost every time.

"Do you have enough time for a drink?" Maggie asked at the end of the session.

"Of course." Wendy nodded. "Like I said, I have plenty of time."

The ladies walked into the clubhouse and were greeted by Jen.

"Good afternoon, ladies."

"Hey, Jen," Maggie said.

"What can I get you?"

Maggie looked at Wendy with a wicked smile. "Tequila?"

Wendy returned Maggie's smile. "Why not?"

After a few shots and several full-fledged drinks, Maggie took the opportunity to turn the conversation to the matter at hand.

"I'm sure you heard about Marco," Maggie said. "Crazy, huh?"

"Ha!" Wendy said too loudly. Then she smiled. "Yeah, crazy."

"Not very many people are sorry he's gone," Maggie noted.

"Probably none," Wendy said, again almost too loudly. "I'm not."

"I thought you guys used to date?"

"If that's what you want to call it," Wendy said. "I still remember the first day he walked into the pro shop. He was wearing a light blue golf shirt opened to the bottom button…I could see an abundance of curly chest hair. He obviously spent a good amount of time in the gym. He was wearing golf shorts that exposed his muscular legs. I have to admit, I've always had a thing for the Sylvester Stallone type…but that guy actually stopped me in my tracks."

"I agree he was really handsome," Maggie said.

"He was also a charmer. The guy had it all and he knew it," Wendy said.

"He seemed like a guy who knew what he wanted."

"And took it."

"How did you guys end up together?" Maggie asked.

Wendy scoffed softly. "He spotted his prey and immediately signed up for golf lessons, requesting me every time." She shook her head. "The guy didn't need lessons. He was really good."

"I believe he's the current club champion," Maggie said.

Wendy scoffed again. "I'm not surprised."

"How did you end up dating him?"

"He showed up for every lesson with some small but thoughtful gift—flowers, candy, a Starbucks vanilla latte. We'd often play nine instead of standing at the driving range. He said he wanted tips on how to play certain holes. What he wanted was privacy. At the beginning I was able to keep it professional…but he was pretty hard to resist. He bugged me every day for my personal cell number until I finally gave it to him. I figured no harm, since I actually gave it to many of my regular clients. Again, he was persistent. He started texting me nonstop."

"That seems annoying," Maggie said.

Wendy sighed. "Honestly, I didn't think so, I actually liked the attention. So even though it was against the rules, I finally agreed to go out with him, as long as we could keep it private. He was just too irresistible…he had me in his spell. I was so stupid, I started imagining it was the real thing."

"You're not stupid, Wendy," Maggie protested. "You're a tender-hearted woman who fell in love."

"I got over it pretty fast, the sex was awful," she said.

"Honestly, that's kind of surprising."

"Marco made love to himself. It felt like I was a piece of gym equipment he was working out on." She laughed at the memory. "He acted like he was doing me a favor by sweating all over me. I let it go on far too long, thinking things would get better; but it only got worse. I became the backup plan, a side thing, the girl you go to when the bar closes and there's nothing better to take home. Finally, I had enough and broke it off."

"Good for you," Maggie said. She smiled affectionately at Wendy then turned to Jen. "Another couple shots, please."

"Yeah," Wendy continued, "I told him I was tired of being his mistress—and you know what that asshole said?"

"What?"

Maggie handed Wendy one of the shots Jen had poured, and they clinked glasses and drank it down. Maggie grabbed a lime to dull the taste of the tequila but Wendy needed to get it out so she kept going: "He said if I wanted to be his mistress, I would have to loosen up in bed. He said I was boring."

"What did you say?"

Wendy scoffed, more loudly this time. "I told him to get the hell out of my house and lose my number."

"Did he leave?"

"Yeah—*after* he took a shower *and* left his wet towel on my bedroom floor." She shook her head bitterly. "Such an asshole."

"Thank God you got rid of him when you did," Maggie said.

"I wish it would have been that easy...."

Maggie watched as Wendy's face turned pale and her lips trembled a bit. She gazed at Wendy quietly. "What happened?"

"A few weeks later, he came back into the pro shop to sign up for a last-minute tee time. As soon as I saw him, I disappeared into the back room but listened to him tell Tim how he had been in Brazil on business. When he left, I came out of the back room, rolling my eyes. I said something like, 'What a dick.' Then Tim tells me I should have never gotten involved with him. I didn't say anything because I couldn't really deny it and if I acknowledged it, he could have fired me for dating a club member, which is strictly against the rules."

"*Everyone* knew about it," Maggie said.

"Seriously?" Wendy asked.

"Yeah, sorry."

"I'm glad he's dead," Wendy admitted. "I just wish I was the one that killed him." Tears started to form in the corners of her eyes.

Maggie reached over and put a hand on her shoulder. "I'm so sorry, Wendy."

"It's not because we broke up," Wendy continued, "it's because the next day he came in the pro shop, he caught me there by myself, which I believe was his plan. As soon as he realized no one else was there he started asking me if I missed him. I was cold and said no even when there was still a tiny bit of my heart that might have. He said he was sorry and really wanted to make it up to me. He said he made a weekend reservation at the JW on Marco Island. I kept my resolve and told him to fuck off."

Maggie was impressed. "Wow, what did he say to that?"

"He just laughed and picked up a pair of golf shoes from the display and asked for a size ten-and-a-half. I took the shoe and went back into the storage room to find it, but he followed me—and when we were out of sight, he attacked me."

"*What?*" Maggie said.

"I begged him to stop but he wouldn't. I thought he was going to rape me—but then the bell on the door rang. A woman and her daughter had come in, they were looking through the sale rack. It took everything I had to keep my shit together."

"Where was Marco?"

"He had already walked out before I even got up off the floor."

"You should have called the police," Maggie said.

"And say what? I did tell Tim a few days later, but unfortunately I had no proof. The cameras in the front just showed Marco following me into the back, and the ones in the storage room have been broken for more than six months."

"Did Tim believe you?"

"Yeah, he believed me all right—he fired me. He talked to Marco, who obviously denied the whole thing. Then he showed Tim some tit shots I sent him during a weak moment at the beginning of our relationship. So that was it," Wendy said. "Done."

Maggie stared solemnly at her friend. "That is so wrong, Wendy, but at least you got rid of him."

Wendy laughed at Maggie's comment. "You would think; but I wasn't going to let him get away with it while I got nothing."

"What did you do?"

"I knew he was dating multiple girls, and that one of those girls was the daughter of a well-known person in town, a connected guy."

"You mean like a mob guy?"

Wendy shrugged. "Sort of, I guess. It's a lot more sophisticated than that. Anyway, it was a guy you don't want to be on the wrong side of. Apparently, the girl thought she was the only one Marco was dating, but when she found out she went ballistic on him. They were both drunk, and she tried to push him out a third-floor window; only, *she* ended up falling out, breaking both legs and a few ribs. She was lucky she wasn't paralyzed."

Maggie drew her hand to her mouth. "Oh my God!" she exclaimed. "That's crazy."

"For some reason, the girl kept quiet. But I just happened to give a lesson to her roommate, who knew everything. I just had to mention Marco wronged me. That's when she spilled it all. I took her information to Marco and made him give me fifty grand to keep my mouth shut. I figured that was a fair price for what he put me through."

"How did you know it was true?" Maggie still was stunned by Wendy's revelation.

"Angie is the one who told me. She was the girl's roommate in college. That's how Marco met her in the first place."

"Marco's sister, Angie?"

Wendy nodded. "That's the one."

"Marco didn't suspect Angie was the one who told you?"

"If he did, he didn't say anything to Angie. I felt sort of bad that I used the information she shared. I was just so mad."

"How did you meet Angie in the first place?" Maggie asked.

"We became friends when I was seeing Marco. It's funny, I spent more time with Angie than I ever did with Marco. He wasn't a very good boyfriend, but he was also a rotten brother. She's actually staying with me now."

"Wow," Maggie said, shaking her head. "You sure have been through a lot of shit." She thought for a moment. "I was wondering where Angie was living now, since Marco's house is still a crime scene…"

"I'm just glad I can move on with my life now," Wendy said, standing up from the stool. "I'm going to go play nine so I can sober up. Do you want to play?"

"No way," Maggie said. "I'm going to get a hot dog and sit here for a few minutes."

"Please don't eat a hot dog," Wendy said, shaking her head. "That's just gross."

Maggie smiled. Then she stood to hug Wendy goodbye.

"By the way," she said casually, "Alexandra is hosting a

dinner party Friday night, she asked me to extend an invitation. You're allowed to fraternize with members now, since you don't work there anymore. I'm sure everyone would love to see you. We're inviting Angie too. You two could ride together." She smiled at Wendy and nodded encouragingly. "It will be fun."

"Sure, I'll come," Wendy said, smiling a bit in return.

Maggie watched Wendy walk out the back door. She seemed a little unsteady as a result of the tequila, or maybe the regret of exposing herself to Maggie.

Maggie sat back on her stool as Jen wiped down the space vacated by Wendy. Then Jen tossed a new napkin down on the spot she had just cleaned. Maggie waited for the new arrival.

"Maggie."

The familiar, accented voice of Rodney caused her to turn.

"Rodney," Maggie said.

Rodney kissed her cheek then sat in the spot Wendy had just vacated.

"What are you doing here all by yourself?" Rodney asked.

"I was taking a lesson with Wendy," Maggie said.

Jen asked, "What can I get you, Rodney?"

Rodney nodded to the bartender. "I'll take a vodka, cran."

Jen nodded in return. "You got it," she said before turning to Maggie. "Anything else for you?"

"I'll have a water," Maggie said.

"Water?" Rodney stared at Maggie. "I would expect at least a glass of wine sitting in front of you."

"Maybe later at the club."

Maggie sipped from the glass Jen had already set in front of her.

"Are you meeting Alex and Britney up there?" Rodney asked.

"Yes," Maggie said. She pulled her credit card out of her back pocket. "Jen, can I settle up?"

Jen reached for the card then went over to the machine to process the bill. By the time she returned with the receipt, Rodney was pointing to his empty glass.

Maggie signed the receipt after adding a generous tip. She noticed Rodney watching her.

"I guess I'll see you later," Maggie said to Rodney as she stood.

"Definitely," Rodney replied with a wide smile.

CHAPTER 7

Miller Lite

Rodney was already sitting next to Alex at the club bar when Maggie walked in at four o'clock. The two seemed to be in the middle of a serious conversation. Maggie sat on the other side of Alex. Fonzie was already setting a full glass of Cabernet as Maggie settled in.

Alex was fond of Rodney. He had been her main bar buddy before Maggie and Britney moved in. But this afternoon Rodney looked like he was about to cry.

"What's going on with you two?" Maggie asked. "Did someone's dog die?"

"Worse," Alex said. "Rodney just found out that he lost his job." She reached over and put her hand on top of Rodney's as he hung his head.

Maggie moved her glass toward Alex but did not take a drink. "I'm so sorry, Rodney."

"I've been with that company for over thirty years," Rodney said.

"How can they do that?" Maggie asked. "Aren't you like the head guy?"

"Obviously not the head guy," Alex said. She slipped her hand away from Rodney's so she could take a drink.

"It sounds like there was a reorganization, most of the

highest-paid executives were let go," Rodney said.

"But that's not the worst of it," Alex added. "Losing his job was bad—but losing his green card is potentially *really* bad. His company sponsors him."

Maggie nodded quietly. For a long moment she gazed at Rodney. Most people wouldn't recognize him as a foreigner, except that when he spoke, he spoke with a thick South African accent. Maggie knew Rodney's life story was interesting; she had heard it many times. He loved to tell it to any new member who would listen....

Both his parents had been doctors in Cape Town, but he had barely known his father, because his parents had divorced when Rodney was very young; his father had started a new family. His mother was also absent more frequently than most mothers. Rodney had been left in the care of various nannies until he was old enough to be sent to boarding school.

Fonzie set a fresh drink in front of Alex and a beer in front of Rodney. Maggie felt it was okay to take a drink of her wine. The three friends drank in silence until the side door flew open and Britney bounced in.

"Jeez," she said, frozen, "it feels like a funeral in here." She turned to the bartender. "Fonzie, what's with this music?" She leaned in and kissed Rodney on his cheek. "Hello, darling," she crooned.

"Hi, beautiful," Rodney said without enthusiasm.

"You doing okay?" Britney asked.

"I just found out my job has been eliminated."

Britney started to say something sarcastic but the next moment decided to be more sympathetic. "Time to enjoy your retirement—aren't you at least sixty-five?"

"Actually sixty-two—but it doesn't matter if I'm not a U.S. citizen. Whatever happens, I'm not going back to South Africa."

"Why do you think you might have to?" Alex asked.

"My company is the one that sponsors me." Rodney sighed. "No job, no stay."

"Can't you apply for citizenship?" Maggie asked. "You've been here forever."

Rodney shook his head. "I should have done it a few years ago. But when I got divorced, I lost my mind a bit. It's a lot harder nowadays. Especially since…"

Alex stared at him. "What?"

Rodney's voice turned heavy. "I'm so embarrassed," he said quietly. "I got a DUI."

Alex gasped. "Oh no, Rodney, when?"

"It was a few months ago; I have a lawyer working on it."

"That's what Uber is for," Britney said. "Or you call one of us and if by some miracle we're sober, we come get you."

"I was at O'Malley's," Rodney explained. "I figured a few blocks…no biggy, right?"

"Obviously not," Maggie said.

Rodney continued: "The guy was actually sitting at the back entrance, waiting for a speeder. I saw him, but I was a little confused when I turned in, and I tried to go around him. Instead of waiting for him to move. He signaled me to roll down the window, and I did. That's when he asked me to get out of my car…and I got to tell you, I had to piss really bad. So I did get out and pissed on the bushes by the gate. The cop said I was lucky he didn't arrest me for public demonstrating or something like that. Instead he put cuffs on me and charged me with DUI."

"What are you going to do?" Alex asked.

Rodney shook his head. "I don't know. Probably go to Canada. I have a Canadian passport. My first wife was Canadian, actually, we lived there for over ten years. I have dual citizenship," he explained simply. "That's another reason I wasn't in a hurry to get Americanized—I would have to give up my Canadian citizenship." He took a long swallow of his beer then signaled Fonzie and pointed to his glass. "Another Miller Lite, please."

Alex smiled sadly. "I've never seen you drink beer."

"I've been trying to keep my wits since the whole Marco thing. Too many blackout nights."

"I totally understand," she said.

"He was supposed to get me a green card. I gave him fifteen thousand dollars, and now he's dead."

"How could Marco get you a green card?" Maggie asked.

"He had some deal with a construction company and he could get it expedited into citizenship."

"And you trusted him?"

"I didn't have another option." Rodney hung his head.

"Maybe you could find another job so you can stay," Maggie said.

"Or you could get married to someone," Britney said with a big smile.

Rodney smiled wide. "What do you say, Maggie?"

"Not in this life, Rodney," Maggie said. Her body was shaking as if she had just received an electric shock.

"You never know, you might like it," Rodney said.

Maggie twisted her face. "Ugh!" Rodney pretended to be hurt.

"I'll hire you if that's all it takes," Alex said.

"Why don't *you* marry Alex?" Britney said. She moved out of Alex's reach just in time to *not* receive the back of Alex's hand.

"Look at us just brainstorming away," Britney said. "Now, Rodney...*you* can help *us*."

"My pleasure. What do you need?" He tucked in his bottom lip and lifted his head.

"We've been trying to figure out who might have killed Marco," Maggie said.

Rodney took a long drink of his beer then motioned to Fonzie for another. "I heard you were caught in his house."

"Who told you that?" Britney asked.

"I'm on the security committee. It was in our weekly report."

"Well, that's precisely how you can help," Maggie said. "Can you get access to the bar code logs for the day and night Marco was killed?"

"The cops have it."

"Of course they do…but can you get a copy for us?" Maggie asked.

"No," he said harshly. "Are you crazy?"

"Come on, Rodney, what's the big deal?" Britney asked.

"We're members too," Britney said. "We pay for the guards and the equipment…If you think about it, the log is sort of our property."

Rodney looked at each of the girls as he reconsidered their request.

"Okay," he finally said, "I'll get you that log on one condition."

"What's the condition?" Britney asked.

"Maggie has to go out to dinner with me."

Maggie twisted her body to face Rodney. "Seriously?"

"Seriously." Rodney put on a genuine smile. "I promise not to bring a ring and get down on one knee."

"That's just a bad idea, Rodney," Maggie said. "People from the club might see us together and think we're a couple."

"Who cares?"

"I do," Maggie said. She folded her arms—like that would ever shield her. This wasn't the first time Rodney had asked her to go out with him, and her answer was always the same: *Neighbors shouldn't date, in case something goes wrong.*

"You want the log?" Rodney said.

"Yes!" Britney answered. She turned to Maggie. "One date."

"Not a date…just dinner as friends," Maggie said.

"Settled," Rodney said. "Pick you up at six tomorrow night."

"You produce the log first, then dinner," Maggie replied. "*And* you're paying."

"Not a problem." Rodney's mood had returned to its normal happy canter.

"What are we doing for dinner tonight?" Alex asked.

"It's two-for-one burgers at O'Malley's tonight," Rodney

suggested.

"Can we count that as the dinner?" Maggie asked.

"Not. On. Your. Life," Rodney said.

The other girls smiled.

"I guess I'm in," Maggie said.

"Me too," Alex said.

"It's the three musketeers," Britney agreed.

"*If* the three musketeers were private investigators," Rodney said.

*

Rodney was fifteen minutes early for his "date" with Maggie. Maggie had begged to drive herself and meet him there…but he insisted.

"So where are we headed?" Maggie asked.

"How's City Fish?"

"Love it," she said. She was relieved the restaurant he chose was close to home. It wouldn't take them long to get there limiting the time she had to be in the car with him.

Rodney hadn't made a reservation; so as soon as they walked in, he headed for an empty booth in the bar.

"This is *so* nice," Rodney said sliding to the center of the booth.

Maggie shrugged. "If you say so."

Rodney handed Maggie the bar menu. "It's good to get out of the club once in a while."

"I'd just rather you not drink and drive, especially since we aren't in the confines of the gates," Maggie said.

"We don't need to go crazy," Rodney said, "unless you want to."

Maggie shook her head. "Funny, Rodney."

"What do you want to drink?" he asked as the waitress appeared.

"I guess I'll have a Cosmo."

"Make that two," Rodney said.

"Appetizers?" the waitress asked.

"We haven't had a chance to look yet," Rodney answered.

The waitress nodded. "I'll go ahead and get your drinks and be right back."

"So," Maggie said, "I thought you were drinking beer now?"

"That lasted one day. I hate having to piss every ten minutes."

Maggie smiled. "Makes sense, since that's what got you arrested."

"Funny lady," Rodney said. "That's what I like about you, Maggie…"

Maggie interrupted him: "I'm supposed to ask you if you would like to join us at Alex's house next Friday? She's hosting a small dinner party."

"I would love that." Rodney smiled wide. "Shall I pick you up?"

Maggie rolled her eyes. "No, I can drive myself. As a matter of fact," she added, "I'll probably just drive my golf cart."

"You could stop by my house for a glass of wine first. I just got a shipment from Napa. There's a great Pinot I really want to try…."

"I'm going over early to help her set up."

"Can I help?"

"Rodney," Maggie said firmly, "back off a little."

Rodney turned away for a moment then turned back to Maggie, frustrated. "I just don't know why you don't give me a chance."

Maggie sighed. "Rodney, it's awkward. We live in the same neighborhood…and if something goes wrong, which I am sure it will, it will only cause unnecessary drama at the club. Neither of us wants that."

"That's not going to happen," Rodney said. He raised his hand and crossed his heart. "Promise."

"Okay, new subject."

Maggie took a sip of her Cosmo as soon as the waitress set it in front of her. The glass was so full she leant over and sipped it in place instead of lifting it up.

"Have you decided on any appetizers?" the waitress asked.

Maggie handed the waitress the bar menu. "I'll have the crab cakes and the oysters Rockefeller."

"I'll take the clams casino and also the crab cakes," Rodney said.

As soon as the waitress walked away Maggie held out an open palm. "Do you have the list?"

Rodney smiled like a fox that had cornered a hen. "Can I get just one kiss?"

"Seriously?" Maggie said.

"Okay, just a hug?"

"Give me the list," Maggie demanded behind gritted teeth.

Rodney reached inside his jacket pocket and pulled out several folded pieces of paper. Maggie tucked the papers into her pocketbook without even looking at them before picking up her drink and finishing it in two long sips.

"Does the report show both the main gate and the back gate?"

"Yes, both," Rodney said. "It's everything from eight p.m. to eight a.m. the day Marco died….Another drink?" he suggested.

"Sure, why not?" Maggie answered.

Rodney motioned to the waitress.

"So how did you end up in America, Rodney?" Maggie had decided on small talk while they waited for their food. And if she knew one thing about men, they loved to talk about themselves.

"I originally came to Miami as an exchange student for my senior year of high school. Then I talked my parents into letting me stay in America and attend the University of Miami. I majored in information technology at the very beginnings of the industry. I was hired by IBM right out of school," he said. "The bad thing is that they sent me to their headquarters in New York. It was freezing."

"When did you move here?" Maggie asked.

"Seems like a lifetime ago. I was transferred here and moved into Boca West. I had a beautiful house, beautiful cars… and a beautiful wife."

"So, what happened? Why are you living at Banyan Tree?"

"My beautiful wife got the Boca bug and started losing weight, paying a lot more attention to her looks."

"When did you notice the switch?"

Rodney frowned, shaking his head. "She would always go shopping or run her errands in a pair of lululemons, hair pulled back in a sloppy ponytail. Then suddenly she never left the house without full makeup, straightened hair—and if her skirts were any shorter…you know what I mean? I knew something was up, so I put a tracking devise on her car. She thought she was so slick by turning off location on her cell phone, or turning her phone off altogether. I followed her and found out she was having an affair with a guy who worked at the mall, at least twenty years younger."

"Wow, where is she now?" Maggie asked.

"Back in Canada where we met, hopefully freezing to death. She took half my money *and* I still have to pay her ten grand a month."

"But she cheated on you. That doesn't sound fair."

"The judge didn't care. The best part is her boy toy took off when her big money ran out. Now she's just a bitter old lady who takes it all out on me."

Maggie shook her head. "That sucks."

"I think you should just give me a chance. I'm a nice guy," Rodney said.

Just then the waitress appeared with two more drinks and their appetizers.

Maggie was hungry. She ignored Rodney and ate her food then finished her drink.

"I need to use the restroom," she said a moment later.

"I'll be waiting patiently for your return," Rodney told her sloppily. He winked at her as she left.

As soon as she was out of sight, Maggie said aloud, "*Time for the old Irish exit!*"

She didn't even stop at the restroom but walked right out the front door. Then she pulled out her phone and swiped until she reached her Uber app.

CHAPTER 8

Dirty Martini

Maggie didn't recognize Doc when he pulled up in a brand new dark blue Dodge Challenger. He seemed to always drive a different car: his father owned the largest dealership in the area.

"Need a ride?" Doc asked, rolling down the window.

"Sure."

Maggie glanced over her shoulder as she walked to the other side of the car, opening the passenger door and sliding in. "I was just about to call an Uber."

"Where's Rodney?" Doc asked. He pulled out, revving the engine for effect.

"In there." Maggie motioned her head back toward the restaurant. "Probably waiting for me to come out of the bathroom."

"He doesn't know you left?"

"He'll figure it out." The next moment Maggie eyed Doc suspiciously. "How did you know I was with Rodney? Were you in there?"

Doc nodded. "I was having dinner with my mom, she's pretty upset about the whole Marco thing. She thinks I should sell my house and move to a different community. We would have stopped to say hi, but my mom isn't a big fan of Rodney."

"I understand."

Maggie sat back, finally able to relax.

Doc turned east. "Are you in a hurry to get back?" he asked.

"I guess not…Where to?"

"How about JB's at the Beach," he said, smiling at her.

"Perfect."

*

As soon as they pulled up to JB's, Doc handed the valet a twenty-dollar bill so they would park him in the front. Maggie waited on the top step for Doc to join her; then they walked through the restaurant and out the double doors at the back. They were fortunate to get the last two chairs at the outdoors bar, facing the ocean.

"It's so beautiful out here…" Maggie said.

"I love it here. If I didn't play golf so much, I would find a condo on the water," he said.

"I was actually looking at condos on the beach when I moved here, but I didn't want to be in a high rise," Maggie said.

The bartender leaned over to them. "What can I get you two?"

"I'll have a Grey Goose and tonic," Maggie said.

"Dirty martini for me," Doc said.

"Ohhhh," Maggie exclaimed, "that sounds kind of good. I'll have one of those too."

"So why did you pick Banyan Tree?" Doc asked. He turned sideways to face Maggie.

Maggie looked out on the endless blue ocean. "I don't know, it just seemed so welcoming and safe."

Doc laughed. "Safe, huh?"

"Well, now there's been a murder, but I think that's just a one-off."

"My mom is going crazy over it. She wants me out of there," Doc said.

Maggie turned to him. "You were friends with Marco, weren't you?"

"Yeah, we used to be friends but recently had a bit of a falling out."

Maggie's interest was piqued, but she kept her voice casual. "What happened?"

"Well, Marco pretty much threatened my family and extorted some money from my father."

"What?"

So much for the casual tone. She could not believe Doc was saying, and that he was confiding in her.

"That's pretty much why my mom wanted to meet for dinner tonight."

"To make sure you didn't kill Marco?" Maggie asked.

"No," Doc said too loudly, "she told me what he was doing to my family."

"You didn't know?"

"I did know, I was right in the middle of the whole thing. It was actually my fault." He looked down at the bar then, for a moment, looked at Maggie. Finally his gaze shifted to the water. He seemed to be staring absently at the horizon. "I told Marco about my family's secrets," he began. "I trusted him, he was one of the only guys who treated me as an equal instead of a rich kid living off his parents. We played in the dart league and golfed together almost every day we could. Marco was a fun guy to hang around with...no matter where we were, somehow the most beautiful girls in the place were sitting alongside us. The nights were always full of laughs...." He sighed lightly but his eyes remained fixed on the water. "It was one of those nights—I think I had smoked a little too much and had one too many drinks—changed our friendship into...something else."

Just then, the seat next to Doc became available. A long-legged blonde immediately filled the seat, distracting Doc from his story.

"Please, Doc," Maggie prodded, leaning over to him, "continue."

"Can you imagine what our children would look like?"

"Really, Doc?"

Doc continued ignoring Maggie. "Are you here by yourself?" he asked the woman.

The woman smiled noncommittedly. "I'm waiting for my friends to get off work."

"What would you like to drink?" He motioned to the bartender.

The woman's smile changed. "Cosmo, please," she said gratefully. Maggie had a feeling this girl didn't usually buy her own drinks.

"I'll have another martini," Doc told the bartender. "Extra dirty."

"Doc," Maggie said. She touched him on his sleeve to get his attention.

The bombshell leaned in close. "You're a doctor?"

"General practice," Doc said, smiling. "My name is Frank." He held his hand out to her.

"I'm Stormy," the woman said with a smile.

"Is that your real name?" Doc asked.

The woman nodded easily. "Yes, I was born in Chicago and my father gave my mom a choice: Windy—not *Wendy*—or Stormy. She chose Stormy."

"Well, it fits," Doc said.

"If you only knew." She laughed.

"I would like to know," Doc said, not noticing Maggie's exaggerated eye roll. "I was also born in Chicago."

"Really?" Stormy asked. "What part?"

"Lake Forest," he said naturally but knew he had just made a mistake.

"No way," she said. "I went to Lake Forest High School. I played center on the women's basketball team. What year did you graduate?"

"We moved when I was in the second grade," he said, "but I'm sure at least ten years before you."

"What a small world," Stormy said.

"I thought you were from Long Island?" Maggie asked. "Wantagh, I think you said?"

Doc eyed her for a moment. "We actually moved around a lot," he said in a hushed tone.

"Oh, my friends are here," Stormy said the next moment, standing from her seat. Doc looked over to the other side of the bar. A group of women were settling at a high-top table.

He turned back to Stormy. "Can I get your number?"

"Sure," Stormy said after a moment. She held out her hand. Doc retrieved his phone. She typed in her number and handed the phone back.

"Thanks," Doc said. Maggie thought he was smiling like a dog in heat. When he finally turned his attention back to Maggie, he said, "Wow."

Maggie rolled her eyes.

"Seriously, Doc? What was that whole thing about Lake Forest?" She shook her head. "A minute ago you seemed upset?"

Doc sighed impatiently. "Can we drop it?"

"Absolutely not."

The bartender placed another round of drinks in front of them. Doc's head was already fuzzy...he had a low resistance. He felt like confessing his transgressions. Maggie was the beneficiary, as she posed no threat.

"You can't say anything, it's just that my family needs to keep a low profile." Doc looked sick to his stomach but took a long drink of the martini. He took the olives and set them one at a time into his mouth, chewing slowly while Maggie stared at him.

"My family is in witness protection. Marco found out."

"Witness protection?" Maggie lowered her voice. "But your dad is rich, how does he stay hidden? I thought witness protection meant low-profile jobs. How did your dad land a big-time dealership?"

"My father is a financial wizard," Doc explained, "but he took a job as a car salesman when we were relocated. He just couldn't help himself moving through the ranks...until one day he owned the place. He doesn't advertise, and everything is done through my mother's name."

"Which is obviously not her real name," Maggie said, "or yours. What *is* your real name?"

"Arthur, or Artie as my mother used to call me," Doc said.

"I got to tell you, you do look more like an Arthur then a Frank," Maggie said. "Are you even Jewish?"

"Yes, we are Jewish," Doc said. "You don't have to change religions in witness protection; but we don't ever enter a synagogue, just in case."

"So, who are you hiding from?"

"My father was the controller for an investment company in Chicago that specialized in getting people to invest in oil drilling in Texas. It was a big scandal called Texas Tea."

Maggie smacked her lips. "I've heard of that."

"That's the problem, everyone's heard of it—and a lot of people had their life savings invested in it. The land where all this oil was supposed to be was just an illusion, it basically didn't exist...the company collected billions without even attempting to drill. The main players have ties to influential families in Chicago. My father was threatened with his life to cover up the scheme, but he kept copies of shadow books as insurance."

Maggie's eyes opened wide. "Your dad's a rat?"

"My father would never have ratted, but my mother's brother disappeared...only to be found hanging in his apartment several weeks later, an apparent suicide." Doc shook his head firmly. "It wasn't a suicide. It was a professional hit... My father received a message that my mother was next. It was pretty easy to disappear, because my mother's parents were both dead and my father grew up in foster care."

Maggie thought for a moment. "Marco found out about all this?"

Doc nodded. "I gave him enough information that he was able to put it all together."

"Because you told him kind of like your telling me," Maggie said, wishing she didn't know any of this. She suddenly felt exposed.

"He was my friend," Doc said.

"Did he tell anyone?"

"No, that's the thing. He wanted to borrow ten thousand dollars. He called it a loan...but it wasn't a loan. He told me that it was security. I have to tell you, I sobered up real fast, remembering being an eight-year-old kid when the Feds stormed into our home in the middle of the night. I remember clinging to my mother's leg, agents in full swat gear combing through the house, carrying box after box from my father's office while my father was led out, still in his pajamas, disappearing into the back of a black sedan. The next morning another sedan showed up in front of our home to take my mother and I to a building in downtown Chicago. We waited in a cold room until my father walked in the door. He ran over to my mother, and they embraced. It was weird because they never showed affection in front of me."

Maggie shook her head in disbelief. "Wow, Doc," she said. "That's crazy...I feel bad for you."

"Don't feel bad, I had a great childhood. I didn't mind trading the snow in Chicago for the beaches in Florida. I barely remember my life as Artie Gabelli."

"Did you give the money to Marco?"

"Yeah." Doc frowned. "But I had to tell my dad because I didn't have that much cash."

"What did your dad say?"

"He was furious. I think he might have killed him—or hired someone to."

"Who?" Maggie was shocked. "Your dad?"

Doc nodded. "The day before Marco died, my father met me here and gave me the envelope full of cash. I had never seen him so distraught. He even took my car and left me the one I'm driving tonight."

"Why did he take your car?"

Doc shook his head. "I don't know."

"When did this all happen?" Maggie asked.

Again Doc said, "The day before Marco died."

"Did you have a gate-barcoded sticker on your car?"

"Yeah," Doc said. "Why?"

Maggie couldn't wait to look at the list Rodney had given her earlier. If Doc's car came through the gates that night, it was Doc's father who killed Marco. She laughed. Was solving crimes this easy?

"I don't know." She quickly turned to the next question. "When did you give Marco the money?"

"I headed to O'Malley's as soon as my father gave me the money," Doc said. "Marco and I were supposed to meet there. He wasn't there, but I saw his sister Angie sitting by herself at one of the high-tops near the dart boards. So I sat with her."

"You know Angie?" Maggie asked.

"I wish I knew her better." He shook his head, his eyes seeming to lose focus. "She's beautiful, with that long black hair…it was hanging loose that night. I asked her where her brother was—and she said, 'Hopefully in hell.' So, then I asked her out. I had tickets to a concert at the Kravis Center. Angie said she would go—but by then Marco was standing behind me…I hadn't seen him come in, I guess. 'Oh, hell no,' Marco said. He sat down in the seat between Angie and I. Then they started arguing like I wasn't even there. Angie said she could go out with whoever she wanted—and Marco said, 'Not with *this* loser.' I finally said, 'Hey, Marco, what the…' He pushed me and said, 'Shut up, *Arthur*!'"

"What did you do then?" Maggie asked.

"I just gave him the envelope and left. People were watching the whole thing and I just wanted to go home."

Maggie stared at Doc uncertainly. "You went home?"

Doc nodded. "I wanted to. But I sat in my car for a few minutes to calm down; then I called my dad and told him the whole thing."

"What did he say?"

"He said he would take care of it."

"You think, he took care of it, literally?"

"My dad just said to stay away from him. Then he asked

me to add Aardvark Pest Control on my permanent access list. I think he was going to have someone search Marco's house for any info he might have that could expose our family."

"Do you think he would really expose you?"

"I don't, but he needed money," Doc explained. "He wasn't going to stop."

"Why are you telling me all this?"

"I don't know." Doc almost started to cry. "I don't know what to do, I had to get it off my chest…."

Maggie sat silently for a minute, confused. What should she do with all the information she just heard? She couldn't help feeling exposed herself….

She looked around, wondering if she was in danger. If Doc were to tell his father that he told her everything, and if Doc's father did kill Marco, was she now in danger? The whole thing suddenly became real.

Maggie excused herself to use the restroom. As she walked away from the bar she noticed Stormy once again approaching Doc. Instead of going back to the bar, Maggie did the old Irish exit for the second time that evening. She went out the front door, clicked on Uber, and in fewer than five minutes was heading east on Palmetto Parkway.

CHAPTER 9

Captain and Coke

Most nights Maggie preferred O'Malley's to the club. It was a place where you could relax in shorts and T-shirts...where you could have a pretty decent meal without enduring the club's restrictive 1950s rules regarding semiformal dinner attire including long pants and collared shirts, even in the hottest time of year.

The Wednesday night wings special and the dart league had filled O'Malley's to the brink. The Banyan gang regulars were out in full force: they took up most of the back bar, likely gathering there to share the gossip swirling around Marco's death.

It seemed as though everyone could recall some transgression of Marco's—*and* who he transgressed against. Maggie held her phone as if she were texting but in actuality she was taking notes on some of the relevant information. She was a little surprised to learn how much Marco was actually disliked. All her interactions with him had been positive—except, of course, that she too had been taken in by his money schemes. Every time he came around, he had always been the first one to buy a round of drinks or contribute to the latest fundraiser. Maggie was sure there had been some catastrophic event that turned Marco bitter. In any case, where was all the money going…?

"I find it odd that the Boca Boozers are just playing like nothing happened," Alex said. The members of Marco's former dart team were all laughing, having a great time, as though nothing ever had happened. The truth was one of their players had been murdered only a week ago.

"It's like nobody is really upset," Maggie said.

"Including his sister, apparently," Britney said.

Britney pointed to Angie, who was walking toward the entrance. The three girls waved to her then moved their empty glasses out of the way so she would have a place to sit.

Angie was dressed in a short jean skirt, white T-shirt, and cowboy boots. Her long black hair fell almost to her waist, but tonight it was in a thick solid braid that hung at the back of her head like a horsetail. Angie was a very pretty girl…whenever she came into the club or O'Malley's, heads turned. The combination of the black hair and her light green eyes mesmerized any mortal, male or female.

Rodney noticed that Angie had walked in. As soon as she was close enough, he reached out and grabbed her arm. She quickly turned on her heel and pulled back a balled fist, assuming a defensive position. The next moment she saw who had grabbed her, and she took a long relaxed breath. She let Rodney awkwardly hug her before she quickly pulled away and made her way to the back of the bar.

"Hey, Angie, sorry about your brother," Billy, the manager, said as she walked past.

"Yeah, thanks," Angie said. The Boozers' table stood next to the big group table. She took her purse from her shoulder and hung it over the back of a chair.

"What can I get you?" Billy asked.

"A different fucking life," Angie replied. "But I'll settle for a Captain and Coke."

"You got it, beautiful."

The manager walked away, throwing a bar towel over his shoulder.

"What the hell are you doing here?" Preston, a team member of the Boozers, asked as soon as Billy had gone.

"The better question is, what the hell are *you* doing here?" Then Angie noticed the three brightly colored darts in Preston's hand. "Are you seriously taking my brother's place on this team?"

"They called me and asked. I don't see why it matters to you," Preston said.

"Well let's start with you are my ex-husband and my brother's dead."

"Exactly," Preston agreed. "He's dead, Angie, and I'm not your ex-husband…yet. The team needs a player, I'm here, problem solved."

"You're not my ex, because I don't have the cash for an attorney and you won't cooperate," Angie said.

Preston shrugged. "Not my problem." He twisted the end of one of the darts between his thumb and forefinger.

"It is your problem, idiot. I want a divorce."

"I say we give it another shot before we throw four years down the drain. Unless you're seeing someone else." Preston looked over her shoulder at Rodney.

Angie turned to see who Preston was referring to. Then she turned back to him, rolling her eyes. He just stood smiling that crooked smile of his. She had once found it charming, but now for the life of her she couldn't remember what attracted her to this guy. Other than his looks. He was almost six feet tall, had blond curly hair and piercing blue eyes. But now he was much too thin, he never washed his hair, and his teeth were stained with nicotine.

As soon as Preston walked away to take his turn at the board, Angie turned to the ladies. "So that was an unpleasant surprise," she said.

"What on earth did you ever see in that guy?" Britney asked.

"I married Preston when I was barely eighteen," Angie explained. "I guess I was looking for the white-picket-fence life

I never had growing up. I had just traded a controlling Italian mother in Brooklyn for a controlling Italian brother in Palm Beach. Marco offered me a job as front office help at his concrete company, and I saw an opportunity for independence. I had no interest in college, nor did I have the funds. The job was easy, mostly scheduling the trucks and light book-keeping."

Angie shook her head as though not believing even the most basic facts of her life; but she was being perfectly truthful in telling them to the three girls. "Preston was one of the drivers who worked for Marco. He showed up at the office every day for his delivery schedule instead of simply calling in. Without fail, he would ask me out, and I would turn him down. It was our daily ritual…until one day, don't ask me why, must have been a weak moment, I finally gave in. But I was specific that it would be a day date as *friends*. I told him to forget about PDAs of any kind. He agreed, and we ended up having a great time. He *is* a charmer."

"I don't care how charming a man is," Britney quipped, "if they don't have a little cash, I can't hang."

"What if they're just down on their luck?" Maggie asked.

"If they're smart enough they'll recover—and then I'll date them. One thing I learned in my life is a man treats a woman equally to how they feel about themselves. If a man has confidence, he'll put you on a pedestal." Britney's own confidence was brimming from ear to ear.

"I'll agree with Britney," Angie said. "When I first met Preston, he seemed *very* confident."

"Sometimes *cocky* can be confused with *confidence*," Britney said.

Angie nodded. "You're right about that."

"Experience," Britney noted.

"He definitely went all out to impress me that Saturday," Angie resumed. "He picked me up and drove straight to PGA Marina—we climbed aboard a boat he had borrowed from a friend. We spent the day motoring up the intercoastal all the way to Jupiter, where we tied up to a dock and had lunch at

Tommy Bahamas."

"I *love* that place," Maggie said.

Angie nodded in agreement but did not let Maggie's remark distract her from her story. "I'm not sure whether it was the calming effect of the water or the perfect weather that put me in a rare mood. It was the first time I felt like I could breathe. Preston turned out to be a pretty funny guy and had me laughing all day…It was easy to ignore the red flags—and there were plenty, looking back now."

"Oh no," Britney said.

"Oh, it gets worse," Angie acknowledged. "Monday morning, Preston came in late, as usual. But instead of a schedule, he received a handshake from Marco, apologizing for the short notice. Marco's was going out of business. I pretty much saw it coming since I did the books—*and* Marco was constantly taking money from the company for his own use. I was actually surprised it all lasted so long.

"Preston got a job at a competitor, and I was hired to work at the casino. The company sent me to Las Vegas to train as a high stakes dealer. Preston came with me. One night after a few tequila shots, Preston talked me into a Vegas wedding, and in a weakened state, I agreed."

"Couldn't you get it annulled?" Britney asked.

"Actually, at first, it wasn't too bad." Angie's voice changed for a moment, turning more hopeful and losing some of its harshness. "I worked a lot of hours, and Preston worked pretty regularly. It was when he was fired from the second job that he seemed to give up. He laid on the couch all day and played video games all night. He never cooked or cleaned but just left a mess everywhere. The final straw was when I caught him sexting some young girl he had met online while playing his stupid video games. That's when I moved in with Marco."

"Now you're living with Wendy?" Maggie asked. But she already knew the answer.

"I am," she said. "She's such a sweetheart."

"Have you heard anything from the detective about when

you can move back in?" Alex spoke for the first time since Angie had arrived at the table. She had been silent up to that point in the conversation but seemed to be taking in everything Angie said.

"Actually, I was downtown this morning speaking with the detective," Angie said.

"Mike Marker?" Maggie asked.

"Yes, that's who interviewed me."

"What did he ask?" Alex wanted to know.

Angie shrugged. "Just normal stuff. He wanted to know about our relationship. He asked about Preston and the status of my divorce. He asked for a list of enemies."

"Didn't they interview you the morning you found him?" Maggie asked.

"Yes, but I pretended to be in shock, so they were pretty easy on me. I knew there would be a follow-up."

Now it was Britney's turn to chime in. "Did he have enemies that you told them about?"

Angie laughed. "I could name a thousand people, but honestly? I wasn't going to give them anything. I played the dumb sister and said that I didn't really know too much about Marco's life outside the concrete business. I didn't even tell them about the few clients who lost money when he closed his business. I don't think any of them would have been mad enough to kill him."

Preston came back to the table. He pushed his way between Angie and Britney.

"You need to back up, buddy," Britney said, moving her chair.

Preston must have just come in from smoking: the air was filled with the smell of tar and nicotine. It hung on Angie's ex-husband as if he wore an invisible cloak.

"Did you hear the lady?" Angie asked Preston. "She said back off."

Instead, Preston leaned in close to Angie. "I need to talk to you," he said, pretending to whisper; but everyone could hear him clearly.

"I'm not interested in talking to you right now," Angie said. "You're drunk."

"I think you really do want to talk," Preston insisted. He looked at the group gathered at the table. "Or I could just talk here in front of your friends."

"Jesus, Preston," Angie said, standing. "If I talk with you, will you leave me the hell alone?"

"Jesus has nothing to do with this but I absolutely will leave you alone."

"Be right back," Angie said, grabbing her purse and pulling the strap over her shoulder.

"What an asshole," Britney said after Angie had left.

Alex motioned her head to the spot near the door where the two of them were standing. "She's giving him money."

"Whatever she gave him must have been enough," Maggie noted. "Because there he goes."

Angie came back and sat back down.

"You okay?" Britney asked.

"Yeah," Angie said. "I can't wait to get rid of that asshole."

"Why don't you move?" Alex suggested.

"Well, I haven't told you the best part of my meeting with the detective."

"Uh oh," Maggie said.

Angie nodded. "Yeah, well it seems like there is some evidence that might point to me as a suspect."

"*What?*" the three ladies said in unison.

"I have to get a lawyer, but I have no idea how I'm going to pay for one…"

"I thought you were at work?" Maggie asked.

"I have a feeling Detective Marker believes I'm the mastermind somehow—*and* I have an accomplice, maybe Preston or his friend Dale," Angie said.

"I'll get you a lawyer," Alex assured her. "I know just the right guy, Landyn Friedman, he was the top of his class at Yale."

"He doesn't live at the club, does he?" Angie asked.

"No, but his grandfather does," Alex said, smiling.

"Of course he does," Angie replied. "But I have no way of paying for a lawyer, especially a *good* lawyer."

"Don't worry about that, I'll take care of it. And someday, when you can, you pay me back."

"Alex, I am so grateful." Tears had started to form in the corners of Angie's eyes. "I promise…I will pay you back."

"Okay, time for another drink."

Britney signaled Billy by raising her hand and circling her finger in the air. The manager immediately understood. He headed to the bar to pour another round.

"I wonder if he can help me get a divorce too?" Angie asked.

"You can ask," Alex said. "If not, we can work on that too."

"Thank you," Angie said. "You ladies are amazing."

Alex smiled confidently. "Just let us know what's going on so we can help."

Maggie couldn't imagine why Alex was so eager to help Angie, though she did have a huge heart under her tough exterior.

"By the way, Angie," Alex said, "I'm hosting a dinner party Friday night and we'd love for you to attend."

Angie hesitated. "I don't know," she said. "I hate to intrude."

"Wendy is coming. You two can ride together," Maggie encouraged.

Britney smiled warmly. "Come on, Angie, help me bring the average age down." She turned to Alex and Britney. "No offense, ladies."

"None taken," Alex said.

"I guess I can get someone to take my shift at the casino," Angie replied.

"Perfect, it's settled," Alex said. "See you Friday night."

CHAPTER 10

Vodka Cranberry

The club had twelve board members, each serving two-year terms. Half were replaced each year to ensure some continuity, but a disagreement between the current president and the treasurer had caused the need for a midyear election. One rumor floating around the club speculated that the rift was caused by a disagreement over the dress code in the bar. Another rumor postulated that money had been spent to refurbish the men's locker room without a board vote. Whatever the cause, six out of the twelve board members abandoned their post. Thus the midyear election had become necessary to replace those six members.

Maggie and Alex volunteered to count the ballots. They had counted ballots in previous elections and found it entertaining. For the most part, Maggie tried to stay out of club politics, but often the issues were debated at the bar. Usually the debates included a lot of false information and exaggerations in order to generate outrage. Whenever the discussions grew too hot, Alex de-escalated by simply walking over to the general manager's office and dragging him to the bar so he could provide an informal briefing of reality.

Britney was sitting in the bar next to her favorite candidate, Brock Adams. She had decided to campaign for Brock exclusively because he was not the typical club member. He had been a professional football player for the Miami Dolphins; now he played golf every day and was a definite contender for this year's club champion.

Fonzie handed Maggie and Alexandra vodka cranberries in "to go" cups before the two ladies made their way to the men's card room, which had been set up as the official counting venue. Britney had no interest in counting, noting it would be a conflict because since she was Brock's campaign manager...even though there was no such thing as a campaign manager.

"You girls make a couple extra marks for my guy," she said as Maggie and Alex walked by.

Maggie smiled to her. "Even if we wanted to, there's really no way to cheat."

When Maggie and Alex walked in to the men's card room they immediately saw it had been transformed into an official office space. The controller sat behind a laptop at a long table at the front of the room. A large lockbox, which had been sitting in front of the reception area for the last two weeks, was now open and empty, its contents spread neatly across six card tables. The piles of pink envelopes sat in the center of the table with only three chairs. Nameplates dictated where each person would sit. Maggie and Alexandra had to switch one person's designated seat so they could sit next to each other. Soon the other volunteers started filing in. It took a while to get everyone in their assigned seats before Jerry, the chair of the election committee, gave the instructions.

"First of all, thank you for helping out tonight," Jerry said. "In front of you is a stack of the unopened ballots. The first thing we need to do is verify each enveloped is signed on the back. If it is not, please raise your hand and I will take custody of that ballot. The next step is to open the pink envelopes and pull out the blue envelopes. Make two piles. We will collect the external envelopes that contain the members signature. When they all are separated, you can open the blue envelopes and pull out the ballots, unfold them, and make another stack. You may then discard the blue envelopes. The person with the number 'one' on his or her nametag will call out the names and the other two volunteers at the table will record the vote. When everyone is done, we are going to switch tables and recount. When your table has finished recording all the ballots, raise your hand and we will come take the tally sheets."

Maggie leant over to Alex and said softly: "I feel like I'm in grade school and we're about to take a standardized test."

"I might need another drink," Alexandra said. She shook the ice cubes in her now empty to go cup.

After the first round of counting, Maggie and Alex turned in their sheets and headed to the ladies' room. The noise from the bar spilled out into the foyer. When they finished up in the ladies' room, they snuck back to the bar, which was now standing room only. The candidates, their friends and families, and other interested members had crowded the room.

Maggie motioned to Fonzie, but he was already putting the lids on the Styrofoam cups. He passed the drinks to the two girls. "How's it going in there?"

"Slow as molasses," Alex said.

The two ladies turned back to the men's card room, prepared for round two. But before they got out the door, Doc stood in front of them.

"How am I looking?" he said.

For some reason, Doc was one of the people who had decided to run for the board. He was totally serious about the whole thing.

"There really isn't a way for us to tell. There are six tables counting…we still have round two to go," Maggie said.

Doc's demeanor suddenly faltered. "Seriously?" he said.

"Well, if our table is an indication, you could be in the top three—but don't say anything. "Just go have another drink," Alex said.

"Or two," Maggie interjected.

Alex added: "We should be done soon."

The girls' inside information had perked up Doc's spirits

again. "Okay girls," he told them, "get in there and count. Use your toes if you have to."

"He's a funny one," Alex said as she and Maggie headed to the card room. "At least he thinks so."

"Why would anyone want to be on the board?" Maggie asked.

"I guess they must be bored." Alex winked at Maggie.

"Doc is still working…he's going to lose any free time he has."

Alex considered. "I don't think Doc works that hard. But I hope he does win, we need some young blood on the board." She nodded to Maggie. "You should run next year."

"I'm retired for a reason," Maggie said. "Britney would be awesome on the board."

"She would rather support the right candidate than run herself," Alex said.

"But she would be great."

Alex nodded. "I agree."

Finally, the counting was complete, and Jerry announced that the winners had been verified. Maggie and Alex returned to the bar, along with all of the other volunteers. Then Alan, the current president of the board, was led into the counting room. He met with Jerry briefly; then they came out together and stood on a small stage that had been constructed for the event. Alan struggled with the microphone until finally he gave up and yelled into the room: "May I have your attention?" He held a spreadsheet in his hand.

The grumbling of the crowd was still too loud. Finally a member who almost nobody seemed to know managed to get the microphone working and handed it back to Alan.

As the names were read, the section of the bar where that candidate and their entourage stood in a tight group would erupt in a small celebration, until they were shushed by Alan. "People," Alan said into the microphone, "let me get through the winners…."

His words had no effect. Maggie did not know the first

three winners, but Britney's guy Brock was number four. Britney was the loudest *whoop whoop!* in the room.

"The fifth new member of the board is Mary Saint James," Alan announced. "And our final new board member is Dr. Frances Cohen."

Doc made a big cheer, as if he was at a football game, pumping a fist in the air.

"Congratulations to all the new board members," Alan said into the microphone. The entire room burst into cheers, some tables a little less enthusiastically, as their names had not been announced.

"Hey, Doc," Maggie called out. Half a dozen heads turned. Calling out *Is there a doctor in the house?* or *Do you know a good lawyer?* in a country club will pretty much get the attention of seventy-five percent of the room. The CPAs, financial advisors, and real estate guys make up another twenty percent of club members. It's the five percent oddballs who are the interesting ones.

As Doc made his way through the crowd, he received slaps on the back and man hugs until he finally reached Maggie and Alex.

"Ladies," he said with a wide grin, "thanks for all the help."

"We didn't cheat for you, if that's what you mean?" Maggie said.

"There is no way to cheat, Doc," Alex said. "You did this on your own. You should be proud."

Doc nodded then pulled his phone from his pocket. "I need to call my mom."

"Wait." Alex placed her hand on his arm, stopping him from leaving. "I'm having a dinner party at my house on Friday, we'd like you to come."

"Sure, sounds great," Doc said, nodding. "Will Britney be there?"

Maggie rolled her eyes.

"Of course Britney will be there," Alex assured him.

"What can I bring?" he asked.

"Yourself."

"How about dessert?"

"It's taken care of," Alex said, releasing his arm. "Go call your mother."

"I can't believe he's so excited," Maggie said after Doc had stepped away. "Seems like a lot of frustration for no pay."

"You couldn't get me involved in that mess," Alex said.

"Maybe when you retire?"

"I'm *never* going to retire. Work less maybe," Alex allowed, "but absolutely not retiring."

"How does your son feel about that? Isn't he eager to take over someday?"

"I think he'd like to, but my company relies on a lot of government contracts, and a woman-owned company carries significant weight when those contracts are awarded. Unfortunately for my son, when I finally retire, he'll be working for his daughter."

Both women laughed.

"When are you going back?" Maggie asked.

"I thought I told you and Britney, the company is closed down for two weeks while we do all the maintenance and calibrations of the equipment and the building. I still have one more week here. Then I won't be back until after Christmas."

Maggie frowned. "We really need to solve this mystery before you go back."

"We—" Alex said, "—will sure try."

Britney made her way over to her two friends.

"We did it!" she said, smiling wide.

"*You* did," Alex said. "I'm proud of you."

"Thanks," Britney said then turned to Maggie. "Your boyfriend was at the club talking to Fonzie earlier today."

Maggie looked confused. "My boyfriend?"

"The detective," she said, taking a sip of her drink.

"He was talking to Fonzie?" Alex asked. "Could you hear anything?"

"No, they were sitting at a table in the back. That new manager who wears bow ties was serving drinks."

"I like that guy," Maggie said.

"He's married," Britney cautioned.

"I didn't say I liked him like *that*," Maggie replied.

Alex asked Britney, "How long did he talk to Fonzie?"

"I don't know." Britney shrugged. "They were already talking when I got there. Then he left after about a half hour or so."

Maggie turned to Alex. "Are you surprised he talked to Fonzie?"

"No, I guess not," Alex said. But she was obviously a little distracted.

"Let's go back to the club when it's calmed down and ask Fonzie what they talked about," Maggie suggested.

"No way," the other two said.

"I'm feeling lucky," Britney said. "As a matter of fact, I'll be right back—save my seat."

Alex and Maggie watched Britney act as if she were going to the restroom but bump deliberately into a young man. She laughed loudly enough that they could hear her. Soon she came back.

"What do you think of the puppy?" she asked.

Alex raised an eyebrow. "The puppy?" she said.

"He's a firefighter. Just finished having dinner with his parents for his birthday. The girl standing next to him is his sister. He just turned thirty," she said meaningfully.

"Age appropriate," Maggie noted, nodding her head in approval.

"About fifteen years too young...but look at that body. If I ever want to have babies, it's with that guy."

"Do you *want* babies?" Alex asked.

"Definitely, someday," Britney said. "Does that surprise you?"

"A little," Alex admitted.

"Did you get his number?" Maggie asked.

"No, I'm going to meet him at Capital Grill."

Britney held a fist out toward Maggie. Maggie held her fist out too then bumped it firmly against Britney's. "You go, girl."

"Have fun," Alex said.

Britney grabbed her purse and disappeared.

"I love that girl," Maggie said.

"She's got everything going for her, doesn't she?"

They talked for a few more moments before a familiar voice sounded behind them. "Well, ladies I have got to go," Doc said.

"Where are you headed out so soon?" Alex asked.

"I have a date," Doc said. "I'm taking Angie to the Kravis for a concert."

"That's great. You two have fun," Maggie said.

"Don't forget Friday night," Alex said.

"Wouldn't miss it for the world," he said, bouncing out the door.

CHAPTER 11

Long Island Iced Tea

Maggie sat at her desk, trying to find inspiration for her new book. She had a bad case of writer's block. Technical writing was much easier for her, because absolutely no creativity was required. Any time she ever tried to add any descriptive fluff in her work, it was redlined by her boss or the proofreaders. Basically, any creativity she had ever had was redlined; pulling anything out of the creative side of her brain just seemed foreign. After two cups of coffee and less than fifty words on the page, she gave up and looked for some inspiration instead. That's when she remembered the list Rodney had given her. She had been so busy that she had almost forgotten about it.

She pulled out the club directory and put a star by all the members who had come through the gate that day using their bar code. The list was actually six pages long. She wrote the letter *c* next to contractors, *e* next to employees. She circled Angie's name because her car came in at 10:47 p.m.—and then again at 4:33 a.m. Some delivery trucks had come through, but the log didn't list their destinations; but chances were these could be eliminated, as food deliveries were always to a specific member. About twenty names were left.

One name Maggie expected to see on the list was Doc's. It appeared as though he never came through the gate that day. It didn't make sense…unless he had not gone to work that day either. If Doc's father came in the gate that night, it wasn't in Doc's car. So why did he trade cars? Even the pest control company that Doc said his dad had him add was also not on the list.

"This list is shit," Maggie said aloud.

All of a sudden she noticed her name wasn't on the list. And she had definitely come through that gate several times.

She laid the pages on the floor, arranging them next to each other. And that was when she noticed: several pages were missing. There was a two-hour gap between midnight and two a.m.

Maggie picked up her phone and called Rodney.

"Hey, what's up, buttercup?" Rodney said. She could hear a crowd behind him.

"Where are you?"

"There's a hole-in-one party going on, why aren't you here?"

"Shoot," Maggie said, "I forgot all about it."

"Your two sidekicks are here," Rodney told her.

"Okay, I'll head down there, but first I have a question."

"Fire away."

"Some pages are missing from the list you gave me the other night."

"You mean the night you ditched me?"

"Yeah, sorry about that. I wasn't feeling well."

"Whatever," Rodney replied. "That's the whole list, I printed it myself."

"You're sure you didn't lose any of the pages?"

"I'm sure."

"Do you think you can get me another copy?"

"If you go out with me again and don't leave in the middle," he said.

"Well, that isn't happening," Maggie said. "I'll see you later at the club."

"What times are missing?" he asked before she could end the call.

"Between midnight and two," she said.

"I'll check it out."

Maggie waited a moment then said, "Okay, thanks."

She quickly went into her bathroom, ran a brush through her hair, and slipped a midlength skirt over the stretchy workout shorts she was currently wearing.

The bar was packed with people Maggie had rarely or ever seen. A "hole in one" party always seemed to bring out people who normally did not come to the bar, allowing them to abandon their normal routines for free food and drinks.

The girls were in their usual spot. Fonzie was busy lining up several rows of highball glasses behind the bar. He pulled out a bottle of vodka, a bottle of tequila, a bottle of gin, and, finally, a bottle of rum. Then he set them aside.

"What are you doing?" Britney asked.

"Getting the Long Island Iced Teas ready to go," he said.

"So many?"

"For some reason every time we have a hole-in-one celebration, it seems like the entire club orders one." He flashed Britney a rare smile.

"That's because they're only allowed to order one free drink—and that particular drink is like four drinks rolled into one," Alex said.

"Exactly," Fonzie said.

"Some things never change." She laughed. "It used to be that the appetizers included oysters, shrimp, pot stickers, and all the fancy stuff, until some of the members were caught bringing coolers and hiding them under the table, filling them up with all the free stuff. Now they serve chili, hotdogs and crudités.

"I think I'll get my P-I license," Maggie said, totally changing the subject.

Britney looked at her incredulously. "You want to be a private investigator?"

"Why not?" Maggie said. "Seems like it would be fun."

Alex shrugged. "I'm not sure retirement was meant for

you. You're sure trying to get back to work."

"I don't think I was ready to retire, but I had to get out of Seattle. The weather was just too wet and cold for my bones. I really needed the sun."

"Well, you have it now," Alex said.

"Okay, wait." Britney held her phone in front of her face. "Here are the basic requirements for getting a P-I license in Florida. First, you must be eighteen."

"Check." Maggie laughed.

"Be a U-S citizen."

"Check."

"Have no criminal history."

"Check."

"Be of good moral character."

"Wait a minute," Alex interrupted. "What?"

"That's what it says," Britney said, tilting her head.

"Who determines what 'good moral character' means?"

"Great question," Maggie said, "but I should pass that one too."

"It's just stupid," Alex said.

"I agree." Britney nodded firmly then continued: "No mental illness."

"Depends on who you ask, but go on," Maggie said.

"No history illegal drug use."

"I did smoke pot in high school."

"I think it has to be in your record…but that was like a hundred years ago, so it probably doesn't count."

Maggie frowned. "Very funny."

"Wait." Britney held a finger up. "No history of alcoholism."

The three women laughed. They each took their wine glass and held it in the air. "No alcoholics here," Alex said.

"I only drink socially," Maggie said.

"You know what they say," Britney added, "rehab is for quitters."

On cue, Fonzie brought a full bottle of Caymus Cabernet

and filled three new glasses with the smooth scarlet liquid. It even poured different than the average wine.

Maggie turned to Britney. "Caymus?" she asked.

"My treat." Britney pointed to the bottle. "To celebrate that I got the job at the Breakers. But I think we should also celebrate Maggie's new ambition." She picked up her glass and said, "Cheers!"

"Cheers," Maggie and Alex repeated.

"Congratulations on your getting that job, Britney," Alex said after taking a long sip from her glass.

"I'm just glad it's so close to home. I'm tired of traveling so much," Britney said wearily. "I need a break."

"We should do a staycation this weekend. Hang out at your pool, call in delivery and drink wine," Maggie said.

"How is that different from any other day?"

Doc's voice came from behind them, causing Maggie to jump.

"Location, of course," Britney said calmly. "Pool and bikinis."

"Nice, am I invited?"

Britney ignored the question. "How was your date with Angie?"

"Fun," Doc said. "Except she *really* hates her ex, she couldn't let it go."

Maggie looked up at Doc with interest. "Really?"

"It didn't help that he followed us all the way to the Kravis."

"He *followed* you?"

Doc nodded. "I didn't see him but Angie was pretty spooked," he said. The next moment he nodded quickly to the trio. "I'll talk to you ladies later, I need a smoke." They watched him disappear out the back door.

The three women talked among themselves and bantered with Fonzie for a while. Finally Britney noticed a woman she hadn't seen in quite a while. She pointed her out to Alex and Maggie. "Isn't that the lady who filed a grievance against Marco for the dog poop?"

"Oh my," Maggie said. "I think so."

Fonzie turned to look at the woman too. "That's one of our 'hole in one' winners," he said.

"There's more than one?" Britney asked.

Fonzie nodded. "Alan Sheffield is the second one."

"Really?" Maggie raised her eyebrows. "I want to talk to him."

"We need to ask him to the dinner party…" Alex said.

The room continued to rotate people as patrons came in for their free drinks and snack then left after consuming their quota. Fonzie's preparations paid off: he had soon used every highball he had staged, plus a few more. He also served quite a few glasses of prosecco to many unfamiliar faces.

"There's your guy."

Fonzie pointed to the door. Alan Sheffield and his partner, Carol, were entering the bar hand in hand.

"Shoot," Maggie said, frowning, "I forgot about Carol. If we invite Alan we have to invite her too."

"I think we're good there," Alex said. "I play cards with her on Mondays. She's leaving for Montana in the morning, her daughter just had twins. I think she said she plans on being gone a month."

"Perfect," Maggie said.

Britney slapped her hands on the table. "Let's get him over here."

"We should get guns," Maggie said out of nowhere.

Britney stared at her. "Guns?" she said.

Alex pointed at the glass sitting in front of Maggie. "You drunk?"

"We need to get a concealed carry license to be legal," Alex said.

"Exactly," Maggie said. "And I know just the person who can give us the class."

"Who?"

"Alan." Maggie let the name sink in. "I heard him talking

to the guys at breakfast the other day. He teaches the class. It's our perfect chance to have some one-on-one with him and actually get guns."

"Do you think he's a suspect?" Britney asked.

Maggie nodded. "Definitely."

Britney was doubtful. "He has some kind of brace on his arm. He couldn't have shot that contraption.

"He wasn't wearing it last week," Alex said. "Remember? We were at Barry Goldstein's one-hundred-and-first birthday. …"

"He could have hurt it when he killed Marco," Maggie suggested.

"I know they had an issue," Alex replied, "but honestly, I just can't see Alan killing anyone. He has a Buddha statue in his yard."

"I think that was put there by Carol," Britney said. "She is *such* a sweetheart—and *he's* more like an uncle who wants you to pull his finger all the time."

"It looks like they are already leaving…" Maggie noted.

"I got this."

Britney stood and moved through the crowd until she bumped into Alan "by accident." She said something the other two couldn't hear, but she pointed toward them. Alan smiled and came over.

He nodded gently. "Good afternoon, ladies," he said.

"Do you have a minute?" Maggie asked.

"For three beautiful women, I have five minutes."

He sat directly across from Maggie.

"Here you go."

Britney came from behind and set a glass of wine in front of Alan then sat back down in her seat.

"Thank you, darling," Alan said, winking at Britney. She didn't roll her eyes but smiled sweetly.

"Did you hear? Maggie signed up for a private detective course?"

"I did not," Alan said. He nodded to Maggie. "Congratulations…Retirement too boring?"

"No," Maggie replied. "I figured it would help me write mysteries."

"Who doesn't love a good mystery," Alan said.

"Rumor has it that you teach the class for Florida's concealed weapon permits?" Britney asked.

"I used to."

"Are you still able to do the certification?"

"I am."

"Can you certify us?" Maggie asked.

He looked at the ladies with a big smile. "I would love to. Why don't we make it a club event? We can put it on the Facebook page and…"

"Seriously, Alan?" Alex interrupted. "Do you really think it's wise to put guns in the hands of any of the card ladies?"

"Hmm, I see your point," he said, nodding. "When would you like to do this?"

"The sooner the better," Maggie said. "Today?"

Alan looked at the glass in front of Maggie. "You can't drink and shoot a gun." He thought for a moment. "Can you meet me at Alligator Alley Guns in West Palm tomorrow morning?"

Maggie looked at the other two. They were already nodding.

"We'll be there," Maggie said.

"Okay, let's meet at eight o'clock. I'll get all the paperwork together and do the class in their conference room; then we'll go to the range and shoot a couple."

"We get to shoot a gun?" Britney said excitedly.

"That is the point," Alan said.

"I'm *so* excited!"

Alan stood from his chair. "Bring ID," he said.

"Hey, Alan," Britney said before he could go, "what happened to your arm?"

Alan hesitated a moment then smiled. "It's nothing big… shoulder surgery I had put off for too long,"

"Ugh," Maggie exclaimed. "So sorry."
"The worst part is, no golf for at least six weeks."

*

The girls showed up promptly at eight a.m. at Alligator Alley Guns and Range. They took their seats around a well-used conference table that had possibly been recycled from an old boardroom. It was thick dark oak marked with multiple scratches and light stains where coffee or water marked its top. The conference room walls were stacked with dusty boxes, indicating the room was also being used as some kind of storage area. The door was marked private but was wide open when they arrived. An old-style coffee pot sat on a card table in one corner: it was half full of black mud. The coffee pot was surrounded by mismatched mugs, a can of powdered creamer, and a sugar bowl encrusted by years of use.

"Anyone want coffee?" Alan asked.

"No thanks," Alex said.

"Brought my own." Britney pointed to the Starbucks cup she had set on the table.

Maggie just shook her head. Truth was, she could use an shot of caffeine, but she wasn't that desperate.

Alex examined the chair she was about to sit in just in case of foreign objects.

"Before we start," Alan said, "do you have any questions?"

"Have you ever shot anyone?" Britney asked.

Maggie looked at Britney. "Why would you ask that?"

"I don't know, curious."

Alan resumed: "We're going to go over a lot of laws and basic information about the care and use of a firearm; but the one thing you need to leave here with is that if you own a gun, you have to be prepared to use it. In other words, if you pull a gun out of your pocketbook and don't intend on pulling the trigger, don't pull it out in the first place. If your assailant sees your apprehension and takes the weapon from you, you're likely dead—or worse."

"What could be worse than dead?" Britney asked.

Alex stared at her. "Britney, really?"

Alan passed out a few pieces of paper and a pen to each of the women. He also distributed the forms they needed to fill out. "Fill these out exactly as it shows on your government issued ID," he said.

Britney picked up her pen. "He didn't answer the question," she whispered.

"He didn't," Maggie also whispered.

The class turned out to be extremely boring but lasted only an hour. Then they were allowed to walk out to the range on the other side of the building. Alan gave them each a pair of goggles and ear protection. He explained the rules of the range and made sure they understood them; finally, he put a gun in the stand in front of each of them.

Alexandra picked up her gun. As soon as the green light came on, she pulled the safety and shot all six shots into the center of the target, a long sheet of white paper with a human form traced out on it. A bullseye stood in the center.

"Wow, Alex," Alan said. "You're a great shot."

"I've been shooting guns my whole life," Alex returned.

"Really?"

Alex nodded her head.

"There's a lot to Alex most people don't know," Britney said. She took aim with her gun and squeezed the trigger. She barely hit the sheet.

"Relax your stance," Alan told her. "Just squeeze the trigger slow and easy."

Britney's next shot hit the sheet, in the center of the human's head.

"Nice," Alan said, "but aim for the center of the body."

"I was," Britney said. "I just got lucky with that one."

Alan moved to Maggie's side. She hadn't even drawn the gun from the shelf, let alone shot a bullet.

"What's wrong, Maggie?"

"I don't know, I just can't do it." Tears were falling from her eyes; as another shot rang out from somewhere on the range, she jumped.

"You have to shoot at least one bullet to get certified," Alan said.

Maggie picked up the gun and aimed the barrel at the target. Another shot rang out. She dropped the gun back onto the shelf then ran away from the range, not stopping until she reached the parking lot. She had no idea what had just happened to her, she was visibly shaking, and she couldn't control the tears. It took Alan a few minutes to get out to her because he couldn't leave the other two ladies.

Maggie concentrated on her breathing. The tears stopped, but she was still shaking when Alan reached her.

"What the heck is going on, Maggie?"

She shook her head. "I don't know!" she said.

"Have you been in a traumatic event involving guns?"

"No."

"Your reaction to gunfire says different," he said. "Were you in the military?"

"No," she said again. She breathed deeply and felt her body relax a bit.

Alan put his good arm around her shoulder. "I'm not sure owning a gun is a good idea, Maggie."

Maggie nodded several times. "You're probably right."

Britney came out of the gun shop, carrying her target like a proud kindergartener showing off her first finger painting. "Check this out." She held up the target with the bullet hole in the exact middle of the head. A few other scattered shots had penetrated the target as well.

"Great shot," Maggie said, but she was still a little shaky.

"You okay?" Britney asked, noticing Maggie's distress.

"Yeah, just reacted a little crazy. No biggy," Maggie told her, "I'll be fine."

"Don't feel bad, Maggie." Alan was still trying to console her. "You're not the only person who's had a bad reaction to guns."

"If you had to shoot someone, you could," Alex said. "I

guarantee it."

"I hope I never have to find out," Maggie replied.

Alex watched Maggie for another moment then turned to Alan. "Thank you for your help today," she said.

Alan nodded in reply. "It was fun. I might have to start giving classes again. It feels good getting out of the club compound once in a while...."

Something over Maggie's shoulders caught Britney's eye. "You're not going to believe this..." she said, pointing.

"What?" Maggie asked.

"If it isn't Charlie's Angels?" Detective Mike Marker said, approaching them.

"That's a good one," Britney said, smiling.

"Are you following us, Detective?" Maggie put on a big smile, feeling a little hot in the cheeks.

"Actually, I'm here to get some range time in," Detective Marker said. "The real question is what are you ladies doing so far from home?"

"Check this out."

Britney held up her perfect head shot.

Detective Marker nodded. "Nice shot," he said. "How did you do, Maggie?"

Maggie frowned. "Don't ask."

The detective nodded again then turned to Alex. "Alexandra," he said, "don't you already have a permit to carry?"

"I'm here for moral support," Alex said.

"Well," Britney said, heading for the car, "I'd love to stand around here all day, but I have a date to get ready for."

"You girls be safe," Detective Marker called as he walked toward the range. "Don't be shooting anyone tonight, okay?"

"Funny guy," Maggie said. She climbed into the back seat of Britney's SUV, which was identical to hers. Britney was already in the driver's seat, messing with the radio.

"Do you feel like that was too much of a coincidence?" Britney asked.

"You mean the detective just happening to show up at the

gun range?" Alex asked.

"Yeah…do you think one of us is a suspect?"

"No," Alex said. "If one of us was a suspect, we would know it. Although, I do think he knows we haven't told him one hundred percent of the truth."

CHAPTER 12

Old Fashioned

Every night was ladies' night at the New Jersey Prime Steak House. Every night, that is, except Thursday nights—when ladies actually drank for free. Free, that is, meaning buy one, get one free. In any case, most of the people who went to the steak house didn't go for the free drinks; they went to meet available men. It was one of those places where the cost of the cars parked in front was in direct proportion to the cost of the plastic surgery of the patrons inside.

"It looks like they all use the same surgeon," Maggie said, studying the clientele. "They all look alike."

Britney squeezed past a group that had already taken the front side of the bar. "They also use the same color of blonde dye and have the same haircut."

"When I get my face done," Alex informed her two friends, "I'm going to California."

"I don't think you need it—but if you do, please don't puff up your lips," Maggie said.

"I really think that *is* a little bit ridiculous," Alex said. She slipped into one of the open seats at the bar. Maggie sat in the empty seat between her and Alex.

"Are you okay?" Britney asked.

"Yeah," Maggie said. "I just can't get anything down on

paper." She picked up the drink menu that the bartender had already set in front of her. "What are you guys drinking?"

Britney scoured the drink menu. "I'm going to try an Old Fashioned."

"You won't like it," Alex said. "Try a Manhattan instead."

"What's the difference?"

"The Manhattan is sweetened with sweet vermouth instead of sugar. But the bourbon is key...ask for Buffalo Trace."

Britney nodded then turned to Maggie. "What are you having, Maggie?"

"House Cab," Alex said before Maggie could open her mouth.

"For your information," Maggie protested, "I was going to try something different."

Alex rolled her eyes and said, "Like what?"

"House Merlot."

When the bartender came over, Britney ordered a Manhattan with Buffalo Trace, Alex ordered a Grey Goose and tonic with a splash of cranberry, and Maggie ordered the house Cabernet.

"What?" Maggie asked, noticing Britney's narrowed eyes. "J. Lohr is the house Cab here."

"You are so predictable." She smiled.

Even though it was ladies' night, the ladies didn't actually figure they would meet any eligible men. It was slim pickings, especially during a hot August evening.

"Hey, look at that one." Britney pointed to a handsome gentleman standing nearby.

"Too old," Alex said. "That guy is looking for a nurse with a purse. And that one over there"—she pointed to a young man across the room—"is looking for a sugar mama. This place is basically a meat market."

"At least it's better than looking at the same old faces from the club," Maggie said.

"Thank God we got here early." Britney, too, was examining the crowd. "It's already standing room only."

Maggie pointed to the far side of the bar. "Speaking of faces from the club…" She nodded. "Check that out."

"Doc and Angie?" Alex had followed Maggie's gaze. "When did that happen?"

"I have something to tell you," Maggie said to her friends. "I think I know who killed Marco."

"Who?" Britney asked.

"Doc's father."

"Why do you think that?"

Britney moved her chair to face Maggie. Maggie recounted everything Doc had told her about his family and Marco's extortion.

Alex nodded. "Sounds like something Marco would do," she said.

"Do you think Doc told Angie too?" Britney asked.

"If he did, he's stupid. What would stop her from asking for money to keep quiet?" Maggie shook her head as she watched Doc skillfully place his arm around the back of Angie's chair, resting his hand on her shoulder.

"Maybe he just wants to get close to her to be able to search the house?" Alex said.

"I think his motives are more carnal than that," Maggie replied. "But I wouldn't doubt if he did tell her. He's too loose with the information, I'm afraid he's going to tell the wrong person.…"

Britney shrugged. "Maybe he's lying about it all. Maybe he told you as a test or something."

"You may be on to something, there Britney," Alex said. "His parents are pretty well known in the community—too well known to be in hiding, especially in Boca. A lot of people who live here also live in the big cities in New York, New Jersey, and Illinois, especially Chicago. It wouldn't be the ideal place to hide. I would think somewhere in Montana or South Dakota would be a better place to be invisible. I couldn't even point out those states on a map!"

"That's funny, I can't either," Maggie said.

Alex agreed. "That's just another question in this whole weird ordeal."

"Should we tell the detective?"

"No!" Britney and Alex said at the same time.

"We don't need to be telling the detective *anything*," Alex said. "Let him do his job, we don't want him to think we're still snooping around."

"You're probably right," Maggie said.

"She is *definitely* right," Britney replied.

Maggie motioned her head toward Doc and Angie. "Should we follow them?"

Absolutely not," Britney said. "Who wants to see *that*?"

"Not me," Alex said.

Britney pointed as Rodney approached them. "Look who else is here."

Rodney acknowledged each of them with a slight head nod. "Ladies." Then he leaned into Maggie. "You will not believe this…" he whispered.

"Okay, what?" Maggie asked.

"It looks like the records from the database were erased."

"Are you talking about the gate records?"

"Yes, I was able to check the records, and there's definitely missing data. Maybe not erased…but the system *was* turned off several times that day and night. If the data was just erased there would have been holes in it. The system was just turned off somehow."

"What are you saying?" Maggie asked.

"Someone in security turned off the reader a few times during the day—probably to test it—and then again between midnight and two a.m. Anyone could have entered and not been recorded. Honestly, it's a cheap system; no controls are in place."

"Oh my God," Maggie said. "Are you sure?"

"Of course, I'm sure," Rodney said.

"Can you find out who was working that night?"

"Already on it," he said. "I'll let you know."

Rodney moved to the other end of the bar to chat with Doc and Angie. Alex watched him go. Then she turned to Maggie. "What was all that about?"

"I'll tell you tomorrow when I get the info," Maggie said.

Britney hopped off her stool. "I'm out of here, ladies," she said.

"Where are you heading?" Alex asked.

Britney smiled. "I have a date."

"Of course you do. You know you need to hook these girls up," Maggie said, pointing to herself and Alex.

Britney shook her head. "You two are too hard to please."

"Who are you going on a date with tonight?" Maggie asked.

"This guy I met named Jay. He's pretty cool—but I think he might be some kind of cop."

Alex looked at her curiously. "Why do you think that?"

"It's just the way he looks, his hair cut, and he's too muscular for his age. He definitely spends a lot of time at the gym."

"So that's a cop look?" Maggie asked.

Britney shrugged. "I just have a feeling."

Alex shook her head in confusion. "Why don't you just ask?"

"I guess I just don't care. But if I found out he was just a dog catcher or something stupid, I might not like him as much. Now, if I believe he's a badass somehow, it keeps my interest longer."

"To be young again," Maggie said.

"No thank you," Alex replied.

Maggie took a long sip of her wine. "I just want to go home, order Italian and watch Jeopardy."

Alex smiled. "I'm so excited for the dinner party tomorrow."

"It's going to be fun," Britney said. "Like one of those murder mysteries in a box...except this one is real."

"I'm pretty sure the murderer isn't stupid enough to just come out and admit it," Alex replied. "But I do love a dinner party."

CHAPTER 13

Veuve Clicquot

Maggie and Fonzie arrived at Alex's front door at five o'clock but there wasn't much left to do. Alex had already prepared the food, cleaned the house, and set the table. She still had an apron tied around her waist when she answered the door.

"How can I help?" Maggie asked.

"If you don't mind setting up a bar over on that counter where those bottles of wine are." Alex pointed to the kitchen's side counter.

"I'll do that," Fonzie said.

"Well then," Alex suggested, signaling to Maggie, "let's you and I go sit outside for a minute."

Stepping into Alex's backyard was like being transported to a small private garden in a remote Italian village. Exotic plants surrounded a stone waterfall. Flickering soft blue lights illuminated the large pool, turning the water into a magical pond. A light screen enclosed the entire area, providing privacy while not obscuring the beauty of the surrounding golf course.

Maggie took a seat as Alex moved around, lighting candles. She finally settled across from Maggie just as Fonzie appeared with two glasses of wine.

"You are a mind reader," Alex said.

Fonzie smiled. "You two aren't hard to read."

"Saluti," Alex said, raising her glass.

"Saluti," Maggie said as they clinked glasses.

They remained silent for a few minutes, enjoying the relaxing environment. Finally Maggie spoke. "That's Marco's house." She pointed to the area beyond the southeast corner of her yard. Alex could still make out the yellow police tape.

"Yep," Alex said, taking a deep breath, "that's his house."

"I guess I didn't realize how close you were," Maggie said.

Alex remained silent.

They finished their wine just as the doorbell rang.

"I'll get that," Maggie said.

She stood up and headed for the door. Inside, she looked out the side glass and saw Alan's familiar grey Cadillac.

"Welcome, right on time," Maggie said.

Alan walked through the doorway looking quite formal in a light grey suit and a white shirt with a sapphire tie. Also, he was holding a bottle of wine and a pink box tied with blue string. Maggie took the items even as Alan looked around Alex's house.

"Wow," he admired, "this place is amazing."

"Alex has done a great job with the place," Maggie said, "I'm sure she'll give you the grand tour."

Alexandra was very proud of her home. Before you even walked in the front door, you were welcomed by an oversized Chianna fountain surrounded by an abundance of planters. The planters overflowed with a variety of colors and fragrances—a teaser for the fuller experience of the backyard. Once you passed through the front door, you entered a magnificent Tuscan resort. Marble statues stood in the corners, paintings from the Renaissance hung on the walls. Even the floors were notable, made from the same wood as the floors at the Vanderbilt's Biltmore Mansion in Asheville, North Carolina. It was quite an unbelievable home in the middle of such a small country club; but Alexandra and her husband had been one of the first members at the club. She would never give it up.

Doc arrived a few minutes after Alan. He parked his golf cart at the back of the house so he could take his smoke breaks apart from the group—Her wore cargo shorts and flip flops, it was the perfect example of the generational challenges of the club's dress code. He had brought a cheesecake and a nice bottle of brandy. After Maggie greeted him at the door—"Hey, Doc," Maggie said fondly—he passed his gifts into Maggie's outstretched arms.

"Alex is in the kitchen," Maggie told him the next moment, "but Alan is out back with the hors d'oeuvres."

"Sounds good."

As Doc headed for the backdoor, Maggie asked, "What would you like to drink?"

"A glass of whatever Cab that's open will be fine," Doc replied.

Maggie took the cheesecake and brandy into the kitchen, where she found Alex sticking her head in the oven while she fussed with some foil-covered dish.

"Fonzie, can you take a Cab and a vodka rocks to the guys?" Maggie asked.

"No problem." Fonzie quickly poured the drinks then disappeared out the door.

"What should I do with this?"

Maggie held out the dessert and brandy.

"Put the dessert in the refrigerator," Alex answered, "and put the brandy over by the other alcohol over there." She pointed to the end of the countertop, where a variety of bottles had already been set out.

Maggie turned, almost running into Rodney, who had obviously let himself in.

"Jesus, Rodney!" Maggie exclaimed. "You scared me."

"Sorry, Maggie," Rodney apologized, "I didn't mean to."

"No worries," Maggie said, "I guess I'm just a little jumpy. I'm just glad I didn't drop this." She held up the bottle of brandy before turning back and setting it down. "Can I get you something to drink?" she asked.

"What do you have?"

Rodney moved a few of the bottles on the countertop around, looking them over. Maggie noticed a bottle of Chateau Mouton Rothschild. She blinked. It was the same bottle—the same exact bottle—she had seen at Marco's. Now it was sitting alongside the other bottles Alex had set out on the counter.

Maggie picked up the bottle and turned it around. Yes...it was exactly the same.

Just then Alexandra closed the oven and turned toward Maggie and Rodney. She saw Maggie holding the Mouton Rothschild.

"Nice wine, right?" she said.

Maggie set the bottle back down. "Expensive," she noted.

"Tell her the story," Rodney said, handing Maggie a glass of Cabernet filled almost to the top.

Maggie turned to Rodney. She was about to ask him what he meant, but then she noticed how fully he had topped off her glass. "Rodney," she said, "you only ever need to fill mine about halfway."

"Well, this way you won't have to keep filling it up," Rodney said.

"If you fill it up too far you lose the whole experience," Maggie explained. "The aroma, the..." She looked at Rodney's blank face. "Never mind."

Rodney nodded. He resumed looking over the selection of bottles. "Tell her the story about the chicken soup," he said again.

Alex shook her head. "It wasn't chicken soup, Rodney," she said. "It was coq au vin."

Alex explained while Maggie sipped her wine: "It's one of my son's favorites. So last year when I was visiting his home in Long Island, I decided to surprise him with his favorite meal. I brought everything with me...except I forgot the wine. Luckily for me, my son has an amazing wine collection; but when I went down to his wine cellar, I didn't see a Burgundy, so I just picked the first Cab I saw. I used the full bottle to braise the chicken, added the mushrooms, lardons, and some fresh garlic."

"Sounds amazing," Maggie said.

"Oh boy, was it *amazing*." Alex laughed.

"Wait for it," Rodney said.

"My son said it was the best coq au vin he had ever tasted in his life. I felt pretty great because he really knows French cuisine. At the end of the meal, he insisted on taking our plates to the kitchen while I sipped my wine and relaxed. It wasn't long before he comes back to the dining room with a discarded bottle of Chateau Mouton Rothschild. He said, 'Mom, what did you do with this wine?' I said, 'I used it in the coq au vin.' He just shook his head and said, 'Well, that was the most expensive coq au vin in history.' Then he told me that that particular bottle of wine cost over seven hundred dollars."

"Oh no," Maggie said.

"Oh yes," Alex said. "I about died of embarrassment. But my son wasn't mad, just shocked.

"So anyway," Alex continued, "a week or so later I get a delivery—and it's a case of the same Chateau Mouton Rothschild, with a note from my son reminding me this wine was to be used for special occasions...*or* my famous coq au vin."

"Hilarious," Maggie said. She took another sip of her wine, wondering what the special occasion at Marco's house had been the night he was killed. Or was it all just a coincidence?

*

Britney, Wendy, and Angie all showed up at the same time, so a blast of young energy hit the house. Fonzie had a drink in every one's hand as they sat outside surrounded by waterfalls and the smell of eucalyptus.

Everyone seemed in a good mood—and they were still busy enjoying the evening when Alex announced dinner was served. When the dinner guests walked into the dining area, salads were already set on plates around the table. Each setting had a nameplate indicating each guest's assigned seat. Maggie sat at one end of the table and Alex sat at the other. Rodney sat at Maggie's right; next to him came Britney, then Doc. To Maggie's left was Wendy and Alan, then Angie.

Alex and Britney had debated the seating plan the night before; this was the configuration they had finally come up with. Maggie didn't see how the seating made any difference; however, separating Wendy and Angie was a no-brainer.

As everyone got themselves settled, Fonzie topped off their drinks—except for Maggie's, which was still too full. She shrugged and pointed at Rodney. Fonzie nodded in understanding.

The salad was a crisp Caesar with homemade dressing and freshly toasted croutons. As Maggie helped arrange the plates she remarked, "No anchovies?"

Alex shook off the suggestion. "We won't be having any of those furry little creatures on these plates."

Soon, the salad plates were removed, and Fonzie served the osso buco two plates at a time. The only other time Maggie had osso buco was at a previous dinner party at Alexandra's, and it had been fabulous. Tonight each plate looked like a work of art: the plate was a white canvas, the veal shank in the center sitting perfectly surrounded by orange and purple baby carrots with a scoop of brown wild rice. Shitake mushrooms and red grapes complemented the dish.

Doc was the first to praise the chef. "This is amazing."

"Where did you get the veal?" Alan asked.

"I get it from Dori's Italian Market."

"I think this is the best meal I've ever had in my life," Maggie said. She wanted to feel guilty for eating the veal, but it was melting in her mouth.

"I think you said the same thing last time you ate here," Alex replied, smiling.

"I can't help it if you outdo yourself every time."

The girls had decided to start with the questions during dessert. So Maggie took the opportunity to excuse herself to use the restroom; she intended to fill her glass, which was finally empty, on her way back. As she passed the kitchen, Maggie set her glass on the counter but stopped when she heard Angie whispering loudly around the corner.

"What do you mean?"

"I told you to wait." Fonzie's voice strained to keep it low.

"It wasn't my fault," Angie whispered.

"It was *all* your fault..."

The next moment Rodney came up behind Maggie and poked her in the ribs. "What are you doing standing there?" Maggie yelped then tried to move back, but Rodney's proximity forced her into the kitchen now in clear view.

Angie stood frozen, white-faced. She stared at Maggie before she broke the spell, rushing past Maggie and pushing her into the wall. Then she disappeared into the hall bathroom, where Maggie had been heading in the first place.

"Geez," Rodney said, "what's wrong with her?"

Maggie shook her head. "I don't know, but I needed to go to the bathroom."

"There's another one down there?" Rodney said, pointing to the opposite side of the hall. "Yeah, thanks," Maggie said, as if she didn't already know where the bathroom was.

When Maggie returned to the kitchen to retrieve her glass, Fonzie had already refilled it. He stood quietly wiping down the counters as though nothing was out of the ordinary.

"Thanks," Maggie said, taking the glass back to her seat.

When she returned to the table Angie was already back in her seat. But she was too far away for Maggie to ask her if she was okay; nonetheless, she could tell Angie's earlier demeanor had changed. She sat stiffly, a forced smile pasted on her lips.

"How is she doing?" Maggie asked Wendy. She realized only now that she had never asked.

"Surprisingly well, especially since the funeral arrangements are done," Wendy said in a low voice. She did not want Angie to hear her at the other end of the table.

"Is she back to work?"

"No, she's been busy with Marco's estate stuff, so the casino gave her paid time off. They even took up a collection and bought her flowers."

Maggie nodded. "Wow, that sounds nice."

Finally, dessert was served. It was even more dramatic than the dinner.

Alex had prepared a warm poached pear bathed in Burgundy wine. It was served in a crystal dish, with a scoop of old fashion vanilla bean ice cream floating at the pear's side. After dessert had been plated, Fonzie came around the table and poured each of the guests a glass of Veuve Clicquot.

"I would like to make a toast," Alex announced. She stood from her seat at the head of the table and held her glass high. "To good friends, good food, and good health."

"Cheers!" everyone exclaimed, clinking their glasses with the guests closest to them.

"And cheers to our amazing hostess," Rodney said.

Everyone again repeated "Cheers!" while clinking glasses.

"Here's to blue skies and green lights," Doc said.

"Cheers!"—and a third clinking of glasses.

"Okay, let's enjoy the dessert before the ice cream completely melts," Alex said.

The room went silent. Everyone dug their spoons into their dishes. Suddenly Britney squealed and swatted Doc away. He whispered something, and she laughed.

"Angie," Britney asked the next moment, "have you heard anything from the police? Do they have any leads in Marco's murder?"

"Nothing new that I know of," Angie said. "They did talk to my almost ex-husband several times."

"Really?" Maggie looked across at Alex, who didn't react.

"Hopefully he gets arrested," Angie said.

"Do you think he did it?" Maggie asked.

"Not really...but it would be nice if they arrested him anyway."

"I wonder who else they've talked to besides us...?" Alex said.

Britney looked around the room. "Has everyone here been talked to?" Nobody volunteered anything.

"I heard it was someone definitely in our country club," Maggie said.

Finally, Alan spoke up. "Well, he did have enough enemies in here…"

"Including you?" Rodney asked.

"Definitely me—but I wouldn't waste a bullet on that loser."

"It was an arrow, so…"

"Have another drink, Rodney," Alan said. "I wasn't the one found asleep at the crime scene."

"I was outside," Rodney said.

"You were probably blacked out when you shot him."

"I didn't shoot him," Rodney replied evenly. "Plus, why would I do it? The only person with a motive was Wendy."

"What are you talking about?" Wendy protested. "Why are you bringing me into this?"

"You know why?"

"Really, Rodney," she said.

"I think we all had a motive," Doc said.

Britney took a drink of her wine. "Speak for yourself."

"You forgot you told me about that business deal," Doc said.

"What was *your* motivation, Doc?" Britney asked, trying to move the focus from herself.

"He was extorting me and my family," Doc said.

"How?" Alex asked, surprised at the confession, "Why?"

"I can't say…but it was serious."

"Maybe your dad put a hit on him," Britney said.

"Maybe," Doc said, "or maybe it was your dad."

"So most of us at this table had some motivation to kill Marco, obviously," Maggie said, "except me."

"You have motivation too," Alex said. "But I'm pretty sure none of us at this table had anything to do with the murder."

"Let's guess who we think did it," Britney said. "Maggie?"

"I think it was one of the card ladies," Maggie said, smiling broadly.

"No one specific?"

"No, I think it was a card-lady gang hit."

"Britney," Alex asked, "who's your suspect?"

"I think it was a professional hit job, so I'll go with Doc's father."

"Doc?" Alex asked.

"I'm going to have to go with Wendy."

Wendy sat up straight. Her face turned red. "I don't even have access to this place, how did I get in? You're ridiculous!"

"You know half the people in here," Doc responded. "I'm sure you could have figured out a way in...."

"Okay, Wendy, who do you think?" Maggie asked.

Wendy sat back in her chair. "I'm going with Angie's husband, Preston."

"Me too," Angie spoke up.

Fonzie, who had been standing to the side, sensed a break in the conversation. "Cordials?" he asked.

*

The group once again gathered outside by the pool, now lit up by alternating blue and white twinkle lights. They chatted easily, all evidence of the tension of their previous conversation gone. Soon, one by one, the guests disappeared, leaving the three women alone.

"I think that went well," Maggie said.

"I was kind of hoping either Rodney or Alan would say 'Let's take this outside' or 'Put up your dukes.' It would have been a YouTube classic," Britney said.

"I don't know anything about that," Alex replied, "but I thought it went well."

Maggie considered. "I wonder if Wendy and Angie know something we don't about Preston? But honestly," she added, "I think we didn't get anything that we didn't already know."

"I would like to know more about what Doc said about his dad," Alex said.

"I'm on it," Britney said.

"Oh, I forgot to tell you ladies," Maggie put in, "I'm going to Seattle on Monday."

"Why?" Britney said.

"I got a writing job a little too good to turn down."

"You can't do it from here?"

"It's actually for a tech manual for a military drone, it's got some classified elements. So I have to write it in a controlled environment."

"They actually trust you with governments secrets?"

Maggie laughed. "Funny girl, Britney. It's a big check *and* all expenses paid. Besides, it will give me a chance to see my family. It's worth the trip."

"Is it really worth it? Seattle is a billion miles away," Britney said.

"At least the weather will be nice this time of year," Alex noted.

"True, the rain stops on the fifth of July and starts back up the day before Labor Day. I think God created the Pacific Northwest as a little experiment. He just keeps it raining and grey until the people start packing their suitcases; then he turns the sun on for two days in a row. The green trees reaching into the sky and the majestic mountains surrounding you three-hundred-and-sixty degrees and the crisp fresh air is all so incredible, you lose your brain and forget about the rain that lasted like forever."

"How long will you be gone?" Alex asked.

"A week. It will only take me a day or two at an actual desk at the air force base. I already have a boilerplate that I use. I just fill in the good stuff when I get there, collect a check, and then back to our murder mystery."

CHAPTER 14

Virgin Piña Colada

Maggie arrived at the Fort Lauderdale airport a little late but made it through security just in time not to miss her flight. She was thankful she had thought to check in on her phone last night; otherwise she would have lost her seat.

It would be a long flight to Seattle, and she really needed some sleep. She looked at the paper ticket she received at the check-in counter: her seat was 3F. She hated the window seat, but at least she was in first class. By the time she reached her seat, everyone already seemed to have a drink; she was probably going to have to wait for hers, until they were ten thousand feet in the air.

"That's me," she said, pointing to the window seat and smiling as sweetly as she could. The older gentleman in the aisle seat looked irritated but got out of his seat to let her in.

"Would you mind if I trade seats with you?" Maggie heard a voice ask behind her.

"No problem," said her original seatmate. As soon as she settled in her seat and was cognitive of what was happening around her, Detective Mike Marker was sitting in 3D, right next to her.

"Oh God," she said aloud.

"If it isn't one of Charlie's Angels, Maggie McFarlin."

"Charlies Angels, huh? Who's Charlie?" Maggie laughed. "Seriously, Detective, are you following me?"

"No, just a really fortunate coincidence, I'm afraid."

"Now I really do need a drink."

Just like that the flight attendant appeared. "Can I get you something to drink before we pull away?" she asked as if she were a fairy godmother. Apparently, she was willing to serve Maggie before the door closed.

"Yes, please," Maggie said as she buckled herself in. "Cabernet."

"So early in the morning?" Detective Marker asked.

Ignoring what was likely a rhetorical question, Maggie returned: "Detective, what are you doing on this plane?"

"Headed to Charlotte," the detective said.

The flight attendant reappeared shortly and handed Maggie her wine. Detective Marker asked for a Mimosa for himself.

"Palm Beach County must pay pretty well if you're flying first class." Maggie smiled.

"Got lots of points," Detective Marker replied. "I'm on this same flight to Charlotte every other week."

"What's in Charlotte?"

"My daughter, Zoey, lives there."

"I'm trying to visualize you as a father," Maggie said, smiling. "How old is Zoey?"

"She just turned thirteen going on thirty."

"Yikes, tough age."

"She's actually a great kid, into school and all that. The only thing that worries me is that she thinks she needs to take care of me. She's also a vegan, so it's tough to go out to eat. Last time I was there, she came unglued when I used a packet of pink sweetener for my tea—and never ever use a plastic straw around her or you'll be responsible for every dead turtle on the east coast."

Maggie nodded. "She sounds very environmentally conscious."

"You could say that. We spent our last vacation at the Outer Banks picking up trash from the beaches. I complained the whole time until she reminded me that at least we were spending time together."

"Smart girl. She'd fit right in where I'm going."

"Hmm, let me guess...San Francisco."

"Right coast but a little more north."

"Seattle?"

"Very good, Detective, I'm impressed."

"What's going on in Seattle?"

"I have a small consulting job at the air force base in Tacoma. My hometown is a small town called Bremerton, across the sound from Seattle. You probably never heard of it."

"I actually know exactly where Bremerton is; also Port Orchard, Bainbridge Island, Silverdale, and Keyport," he said.

"Navy?"

"Marines. I was stationed at Keyport for three years."

"Impressive," Maggie said.

"So how on earth did you go from Bremerton, Washington, to South Florida? Don't take offense," Detective Marker told her, "but you just don't seem like the Boca type."

"I traded grey skies for blue skies. I couldn't face another depressing winter there. It was a choice between Zoloft or sunshine. I have to ask you the same thing, you're also not the Boca type. What brought you there?"

The detective shifted in his seat. "I originally came down to help take care of my parents, who have both since passed. I decided to stay, fix up the place, and was promoted to detective. Besides my daughter, I had nothing keeping me in North Carolina."

Maggie looked at the detective's left hand, which was now absent of a ring. "What about your wife?"

"I'm not married," Detective Marker said, immediately noticing the confusion on Maggie's face. "I wear the band at work; for some reason, people trust a married man more than a single cop. Don't ask me why, it's a psychological thing."

"Really?"

Maggie was pleasantly surprised but needed to quickly change the subject before she embarrassed herself.

"It's really a long story," Detective Marker said.

Maggie looked at her smart watch. "We still have another two hours until we reach your destination and my connection in Charlotte."

Whether it was the mimosa or the connection Maggie felt beginning to establish itself between them, Detective Marker took the invitation and spilled his guts. Surprisingly.

"The only thing I ever wanted was to get out of the small town I grew up in. I was attending the University of North Carolina, I was studying forensic accounting. I'd just finished my second year when the money ran out, so I sat down with a marine corps recruiter. I told him about my studies in forensic accounting but all he heard was *forensic* and stuck me in law enforcement. I didn't complain and ended up as a military policeman stationed at Keyport."

"How did you end up in Boca?" Maggie asked.

"My sister Joanie was getting in trouble and my parents were having a hard time; they had us later in life. So I left the marines and moved home to help. I got a job with the Rowen County sheriff's department. As soon as Joanie graduated high school, my parents moved to Century Village in Boca Raton. My sister got married and had her first child before her twenty-first birthday but then she actually straightened up, finished college, and got a great job at the bank. She's been there ever since."

"That's wonderful. Is that when you moved to Boca?" Maggie asked.

"Not quite. I ended up marrying my old high school girlfriend, but it was a turbulent relationship from the very beginning. We almost divorced less than six months into the marriage, when we found out she was pregnant. We made an effort for the baby's sake—but oil and water just don't mix. The only good thing that came out of it is my daughter Zoey. She really is the joy of my life."

Maggie watched as Detective Marker pulled out his phone and swiped a few times. He showed Maggie the screen. Zoey was a beautiful girl with eyes that matched her father's.

"She is beautiful, Detective Marker," Maggie said.

"Inside and out," Detective Marker replied, smiling proudly. "She might be the only thing I've done right in my whole life. But please," he said, putting the phone away, "call me Mike."

Maggie paused, considering. Then she said, "I'm surprised you live in Boca instead of Charlotte."

"Zoey actually lives in a small town called Faith…I say 'Charlotte' for the same reason you say 'Seattle': no one would have a clue where I was referring to. But a few years ago, my mom got sick, and my dad needed my help. I was commuting back and forth until I was served with divorce papers, so I moved in full time with my parents and took a job with Palm Beach. Within the next few years, I was made detective and both my parents passed."

"Mike, I'm so sorry…" Maggie said. She had begun to realize the detective was actually a good man.

"It is what it is. I do have my sister, who is also my best friend," Mike said.

Maggie smiled. "Aw, that's sweet…"

"She's such a great girl," Mike continued. "I feel so bad for her. She's had a rough time the last few years. She has two kids, and her husband left her about a year ago."

"How old are the kids?"

"One is in high school and the other will be starting fourth grade in the fall."

"Big gap."

"Her marriage had been tough the whole time; so I think the second one might have been an accident. But that baby girl has been a blessing to our whole family, so everything for a reason."

The detective shifted in his seat again and finished off his mimosa. "So now you know my whole story, what's yours?"

Maggie again looked at her watch. "We definitely don't have time for that," she said.

"Okay, so tell me," Mike said, staring into her eyes, "what were you girls doing at the gun range, the other day?"

"Shooting guns."

"Really, at a gun range? Imagine that."

"I don't know if you've heard, Detective, there's a murderer running around our neighborhood."

"No, I hadn't heard." He sat back and with his next breath said: "How well do you know your buddies?"

"My buddies?"

"Your girls?"

"Well, that was a quick switch into detective mode." Maggie took a sip of her wine. "We interviewed all the lead suspects at our dinner party last night."

"You did what?"

"It was harmless, I really don't think any of those people had anything to do with Marco's murder."

"You know that both your friends have lawyers representing them?"

Maggie shook her head. "No, but I'm sure they both have nothing to hide....I'm sure Alex is only protecting her business since Marco was involved, and Britney is just protecting herself because of the hotel." She stared into Mike's eyes. "I know you know all this."

Mike shook his head. His face had flushed, as if he were holding in a lot of foul words.

"Seriously, are you going to arrest me for having dinner with my friends?" Maggie asked.

"*Are* Wendy and Angie your friends?"

"Of course they are," Maggie replied. "Well, sort of..."

"Maggie, I'm being serious here. You need to stay away from this thing. There are things you don't know—and I can't tell you. You're a nice lady. I don't want to see you get hurt."

Maggie smiled gently. "I'm a lot tougher than you think, Detective Marker."

"Is that why you froze on the gun range?"

Maggie started. "Oh my God...how do you know that?"

Mike shrugged. "I'm a detective. Plus I've known Alan for years. We shoot together all the time."

"Isn't Alan a suspect?"

"No, he's not...But again, can you stay out of my investigation?"

Maggie gazed quietly at Detective Marker, still in disbelief. "Wow, I would have thought Alan would be at the top of your list...."

"Maggie, again..."

"I know, stay out of it. But I have to tell you one thing I might not have told you about Marco."

Mike nodded. "Okay?"

"He sort of took some money from me and didn't pay me back."

"Yeah, I know.

Maggie blinked. "You do?"

"Yeah, again I am a detective."

"Am I a suspect?" Maggie asked.

"No." Mike smiled. "If the list included all those he owed money, it would be a mile long."

"You're probably not supposed to be telling me this..." Maggie said.

"I don't think that curious brain of yours will stop anytime soon," Mike replied, "so let's make a deal."

"Okay." Maggie nodded.

"You quit snooping around this case, and when you get your private investigator license, I'll send some work your way."

Maggie stared at Mike incredulously before recovering. "Number one, I have to have two years' experience before I can practice—and number two...how the heck did you know I was thinking about getting my P-I license? And don't say 'I'm a detective.'"

Mike smiled mysteriously. "I have my ways."

"Really?"

"Yes, really. But I'll make you another deal…If you want to try again at the gun range, I'll take you after hours and we'll start with a much smaller gun."

Maggie turned away. "I honestly can't explain what happened to me that day."

"Don't be too hard on yourself," Mike told her, "it happens. You just need to get right back on that horse."

Maggie paused, then turned back to Mike and smiled. "I'll think about it."

"You have my cell number, it's on the back of the card I gave you."

Maggie rolled her eyes then shook her head.

"Just remember," Mike said, "a victim is not always innocent…but a vigilante is not a remedy to a crime. It also *is* a crime."

"What's that supposed to mean?" Maggie asked.

Mike placed his hand on Maggie's shoulder. "Listen," he told her seriously, "you need to stop with this amateur sleuthing. This is a real murder, not a television show."

Maggie looked into Mike's eyes again. She nodded then shrugged his hand gently from her shoulders. Just then the pilot announced their arrival at Charlotte Douglas International Airport. Seatbacks came back to their original positions and tray tables went up. The two remained silent until the plane landed. They got through the breezeway together, pausing before going their separate ways.

"Safe travels, Maggie McFarlin," Mike said with a grin.

"Good luck with your daughter, Detective Mike Marker," Maggie returned warmly.

She turned toward the D gates, measuring each step, unsure if the lightness she was feeling were wine induced or the aftereffects of Mike Marker.

She reached the gate for her connecting flight to Seattle, only to find it was delayed two hours. She sat in a chair near the gate and pulled out her Kindle just as her phone buzzed. She was surprised to see a text from the detective.

> Mike: *Sorry your flight is delayed, I would stay and keep you company but I promised to pick my daughter up by 3.*

"*That would have been nice,*" Maggie said to herself and quickly texted back.

> Maggie: *No problem TTYL.*

Maggie needed a drink and found the nearest bar. She ordered a virgin piña colada. She figured she'd now had enough alcohol for the day and wanted to keep a clear head.

She pulled out her phone again and searched for links to online private investigator training sites. When she found one that looked like it would work she signed up.

The next five days flew by. Maggie picked up the engineering drawings from her the department head and locked herself in an empty conference room....Words flowed remarkably easily whenever she was engaged in writing a document that involved engineering terms. When she was a college student, she had wanted to study literature or journalism, but her scores in mathematics were so high, her school counselor had talked her into undertaking an electrical engineering degree at the University of Washington.

But the factor that had determined the course of her professional life was an offer from Boeing to pay for her degree in exchange for working for them for at least five years. She really hadn't known how she was going to pay for college, so it was a win-win. Thirty years later, she was able to retire when she was only fifty-five years old, after a career working as a junior engineer until an opportunity as a technical writer had become available.

Those days, when she had gotten up at four in the morning, choosing the Southworth Ferry route rather than fighting

I-5 traffic, seemed like a different life—one she had traded long ago for a life of sunshine and golf. After returning the drawings and emailing her doc to her former boss, Maggie McFarlin packed her bags and summoned an Uber, feeling very fortunate.

CHAPTER 15

Johnny Walker Blue

Britney picked Maggie up from the Fort Lauderdale airport late in the afternoon.

"Welcome back," Britney said as Maggie slid in the passenger side.

"Thanks, but you really didn't have to pick me up, I could have grabbed an Uber."

"I was working right down the street," Britney said. "Plus, I missed you."

"Aw, thanks," Maggie said.

"I'm really glad you're back, things are a little crazy here."

Maggie stared at her. "What have I missed?"

"Nothing at the club, just work."

"I'm glad to be back. The Seattle weather sucks, even in summer."

Britney smiled. "I want to go with you next time."

"I would love that...we can stay at the Alderbrook Inn and go hiking at Staircase," Maggie said.

"No staircases for me," Britney replied.

"Not that kind of staircase. Staircase is a hiking trail in the Olympic Mountains."

"Ah, I see." She nodded once. "That sounds fun."

"Maybe we can spot Bigfoot," Maggie said, smiling.

"Maybe not," Britney said. "But hey, speaking of 'big' stuff, would you mind if we stop and see my dad at Boca Big's? He's been calling me nonstop for the last few days."

"Boca Big's?" Maggie asked. "But no, I don't mind."

"It's a cigar bar in a strip mall right off of Palmetto Parkway."

A short while later, Britney and Maggie walked through the door of Boca Big's Cigar Bar. Britney stopped just past the counter. She peered through the thin cloud of smoke until she spotted her father. He was sitting on an overstuffed brown leather chair in front of a dark walnut coffee table. Maggie imagined the room was what she might have encountered had she traveled across time and space, exiting one dimension and entering another....The room was open, but the voices were muted, as if the smoke and the thick leather furniture absorbed the occupants' conversation.

Several groups of men were sitting around small tables, each with a cigar in some variable stage of consumption. Flakes of ash covered every surface. Several large-screen televisions were mounted high on each wall. Most of the televisions were set to a sporting event of some kind, including a horse race taking place halfway around the world.

Britney and Maggie walked up to where Britney's father sat in the leather chair, talking to another man. Maggie felt underdressed: the dress code seemed to be from a time before women burned their bras or started wearing sensible shoes. The man talking with Britney's father was the first to spot the two women. He stood up to greet them.

Vincent Cabrelio was like an uncle to Britney; he had been a part of her life since she was born. He was a big guy and looked a lot like Britney's father.

Joe, Britney's father, and a well-known real estate developer in Palm Beach County, stood about five foot ten and weighed maybe three hundred pounds. He had big brown eyes with thick black eyelashes. He was a handsome man...but it was likely those eyes that had won her mother's heart.

Joe was the reason Britney was living in Banyan Woods Country Club. He had convinced her that it was a great investment and would greatly increase in value, even in the very short term. Britney agreed to the arrangement, figuring her father had some inside information.

"Ladies."

Vincent smiled, opening his arms to gather Britney in an enthusiastic hug. Like Joe, he was well dressed, sporting a jacket and slacks, but no tie. His hair was black and slicked back across his balding head. His cologne reached Maggie before she leaned in to receive the obligatory hug.

Joe kissed Britney's forehead after Vincent released her; then he nodded to Maggie.

Vincent moved his drink to the small table in front of the oversized chair beside Britney's father, leaving the small couch open for the girls to sit. Then a stout man approached them. "You need a drink?" he asked, standing in front of them.

"Yes, please," Britney said. She turned to her father. "What are you guys drinking?"

"Johnny Walker Blue," Joe said.

"I'll have one of those," Britney said.

Maggie said, "I'll have a glass of Cabernet."

"She'll have the same as us," Britney said, raising her hand and moving her finger in a circle.

"Seriously?" Maggie looked at Britney wide eyed.

"Pull up your big girl panties, woman," Britney said, smiling.

Maggie resigned herself to her friend's protocols and sat back on the couch.

The television was suddenly louder than it had been. Maggie looked over and saw the man who had taken her drink order with a remote in his hand, standing by a group of smokers surrounding the television broadcasting the horse race. Everyone in the group was now standing, eyes glued to the set in anticipation. Joe and Vincent ignored the group and leaned close to each other. Britney took the hint: she also leaned in close.

Maggie couldn't hear much of what was said—only *"She's cool,"* from Britney.

The horse racing group suddenly shouted then sat talking excitedly among themselves about whichever horse had placed or won. Maggie couldn't really make it out, and she was much more interested in the conversation at her own table, where she was considered *"cool."*

As soon as the rocks glass was placed in front of her, Maggie took a deep breath and followed Britney's lead. She took her glass in hand and had a good sip.

The moment the drink hit her lips, Maggie felt hot. It was a fire. Not hot enough to burn, but the liquor left a trail as it slid from her tongue and traveled down her throat. She could feel it finally reach her stomach, where it quickly dispersed to every part of her body. She felt electricity in her fingertips, as well as in the tips of her toes.

Britney smiled, watching Maggie's reaction. "Good stuff, huh?"

Maggie nodded.

Joe turned to Britney, ignoring Maggie's red face. "What did the cops ask?"

Britney shook her head. "They really didn't ask me anything. I don't think they made the connection."

"They may not have made the connection but were pretty sure they figured out Marco was part of the Ibis Hotel project," Vincent said. "Our guy at the FBI said they had a lead."

Maggie felt her pulse quicken. Vincent was obviously more than a typical real estate attorney.

"I found this at his house." Britney pulled out the small notebook that she had taken from Marco's house and handed it to Vincent. Maggie held back her shock; she had no idea Britney had taken anything from Marco's house, although she did remember seeing Britney holding the notebook.

Vincent flipped through the first few pages. "Shit!" he said, "I can't believe they didn't find this."

"Honestly," Britney said, "it looked like they hadn't taken

anything out of the house except the body."

"I can't believe you went in there with those two women," Joe said.

"They are the best cover ever; the cops just think we're a bunch of nosy neighbors."

Maggie felt a little confused: they were speaking as if she wasn't sitting right next to them. She took the opportunity to remind them of her presence by taking another sip of her drink. This time it went down a lot easier.

"These are all our contacts on the project," Vincent said. He reached across and handed the notebook to Britney's father. "I mean the full list."

"Can I move now?" Britney asked, looking at the two men.

"Absolutely not," Joe said. "You have to stay put for a little bit longer."

Maggie became more confused. Britney had moved to Banyan Tree Country Club to secure an investment. Did she have more information on Marco than she had let on?

"Marco's dead," Maggie said. "You really don't need me there anymore."

"We still need your eyes and ears until this whole thing is over," Vincent replied.

"I feel like I live at an old folk's home," Britney said. After a moment she looked at Maggie. "Not you, of course."

"Of course," Maggie said. She had reached the bottom of her glass and felt a little light headed.

"Don't be ridiculous," Joe told his daughter.

Britney replied, "Dad, I'm serious. Just yesterday I was waiting for the valet to bring my car when an older Cadillac pulls up and an old lady gets out the passenger side. The valet was confused because he had just put her in the car a few minutes before. The valet asks if there's a problem. She says yes. The woman tells the valet that she got into the car with the wrong husband. When they reached the driveway she looks over at the guy and says, 'Hey, this isn't my house,' so the guy looks over at her and says, 'Hey, you're not my wife.'" The two men started laughing, but Britney shook her head. "You can't make this shit up. I'm twenty-nine years old, I should be living at the beach instead of in senior living."

"You're being dramatic," Joe said. "It's not only seniors that live there. You got a good life, kid, enjoy it."

"What about the project?" she said. "My name is in that book."

Britney pointed to the notebook, which was still in her father's hand.

"Don't worry," her father said, waving her concerns away, "we'll take care of it."

"Has anyone talked to Brandon?" Britney asked. "Did he rat?"

"That's the rumor, but nothing for sure," Joe said.

"Since the government canceled all the E-B-5 visas issued as part of the project, there are some pretty angry investors," Vincent said.

"Can they track any of the contractors that were already paid?" Britney asked.

"I don't think there are any electronic records of the second set of books. This could be it." Joe held up the notebook. "Everything in our offices has been shredded."

"Some of those expenditures were legit," Britney noted.

"Yeah, tell that to some Brazilian who invested a couple mil and got nothing for it," Joe said. "I don't think they'll care: legit or not, they're going to want their money back."

"We're not worried about the cops," Vincent said.

Britney frowned and shook her head. "Shit," she said. She turned to her dad. "Any bites on the property?"

"We got an offer from a British investment firm last week: forty-five million."

Britney's eyes brightened. "That's good, right?"

"Good for me," Joe said, smiling.

"Hopefully no one puts two and two together," Britney said.

"Hey, the government handed me this listing. Boca is a

small town, so coincidences are just that. Coincidences. No reason we can't make a buck off a legit real estate sale."

"It also helps when you got friends in the government." Vinnie laughed.

"Well, don't forget me when payday comes," Britney said. She stood, a little wobbly from the whiskey.

"You're my baby girl, daddy would never forget you."

Vincent nodded at Britney. "Uncle Vinny's got your back, kid."

Britney smiled then leaned over to Uncle Vinny, kissing him on both cheeks. She repeated the ritual with her father.

"Maggie," Vinny said. He turned to Maggie and looked her squarely in the eyes. "You realize this is just business, right?"

Maggie again felt her pulse quicken. She put all her effort into remaining level headed. "Honestly, I have no idea what you guys are talking about—and I don't want to know."

Vinny eyed Maggie for a moment then turned to Britney. "By the way," he said, "your friend Alex has some connections to some mutual investors in Brazil."

Britney stared at him. "What kind of connections?"

"There's a company called Avioa de Primo's, it's a Brazilian aircraft company."

"That doesn't seem odd…Alex's company sells aircraft parts all over the world."

Her father nodded. "Maybe it's just coincidence."

Britney seemed to believe her father was satisfied with that explanation, but Maggie wondered if Joe hadn't dismissed his concerns a little too casually. She didn't have time to consider the matter for much longer though: Britney held her hand out to help Maggie up. Maggie's legs stuck to the leather couch as she stood up, causing her to experience a peeling sensation.

"Well, you guys be good, if that's even possible," Britney said over her shoulder. She walked out the door, feeling the electricity building in the air.

"What the heck?" Maggie asked Britney as they climbed into the car.

"Sorry, I should have given you a heads up."

"What's an E-B-5 thing? What was in that notebook? How are you involved?" Maggie fired off each question without giving Britney time to answer.

"My ex, Brandon, was involved with the building project, which had been registered as a government project—meaning it allows foreign investors to get a shortcut to citizenship here in the states. If they invest enough money in a project that creates ten jobs, they get five green cards...and of course they're investors, so they also get a share of the profits. The problem is, the building managers took the money from the investors—but instead of spending it all on the project, they bought expensive cars, houses, jewelry, you name it. All *very* illegal."

"And you were involved?" Maggie asked.

"Well," Britney said, "sort of, but not really."

"That makes perfect sense." Maggie rolled her eyes.

"I was hired to do the lobby design, and I got a pretty big advance. I had no idea what was going on until Marco told me that one of his investors was suspicious. He said he had a list of all the contractors who were paid and didn't do anything."

"Why didn't you just give the money back?" Maggie asked.

"I would have if I had it, but Brandon spent the money. I never really had it, but if I'm exposed, I'll lose my license and, worse, my reputation. Basically everything I've built up. I won't recover."

"Was Marco extorting you?"

"Yes." Britney nodded. "I gave him ten grand, but I was sure he was going to ask for more. That's when I had to go to my dad. That's the real reason I live in Banyan Tree. My father wanted me to stay close."

"Wasn't Marco suspicious when you moved in?"

"Not at all, he's the one who told me what a great deal it was to live there. He said I would enjoy the country club lifestyle. He actually thought I took his advice by moving in there. Keep your enemies close, you know," Britney said, smiling.

"Wow, Britney." Maggie shook her head incredulously.

"Did you tell the detective any of this?"
 "I told him to talk to my lawyer," Britney said.

CHAPTER 16

Peach Schnapps

The next morning Maggie arrived fifteen minutes late for her hair appointment. She was so tired from traveling across country twice in a week her brain still hadn't synchronized with the east coast time zone. She considered canceling, until she looked in the mirror and saw the wide grey path along the top of her scalp. She had already put off the appointment for two weeks and had reached the point where she would have to wear a hat if she wanted to go out in public.

The chemical smell of a keratin treatment almost knocked her over as soon as she walked through the door. It was like the old days when she used to perm her hair. The smell of the solution applied to the tightly wound rods. The perm solution lingered for days, until you could finally wash your hair. Now keratin was an expensive chemical treatment you could use to straighten your hair. Maggie wondered why women—and even men—went to such drastic lengths to change their natural look. But even if it was illogical there was no way she was going to let her hair turn grey.

"You look like you've been run over by a truck."

Tanya appeared just before Maggie sat in the waiting area.

"Nice to see you too," Maggie said, forcing a smile. "Just tired."

"Come with me."

Tanya pulled Maggie down the short hall then through a door to her private station.

"Sit here and I'll get you something to drink."

She helped Maggie into the black, oversized smock then disappeared around the corner.

Maggie was relieved. The room took her out of the salon and set her down in a mini-oasis. Plants and waterfalls surrounded the room. Spanish guitar music played softly on small speakers. Maggie melted into the chair, almost forgetting where she was. Only when she opened her eyes and found herself staring straight into a giant mirror framed in bright lights, did she get the full effect of what Tanya saw.

She was a mess. Her hair was pulled back into a sloppy ponytail, and she hadn't put on makeup: the dark circles under her red eyes looked as if she had been in a fight. The only positive was the absence of wrinkles. Maggie had had some work done on her eyes, but unlike many of her friends, she hadn't had to go down the Botox road quite yet.

Tanya came back and handed Maggie a champagne glass.

"Oh Lord," Maggie said, wishing for coffee instead.

"Drink it," Tanya told her, moving behind Maggie. "It's my special pick-me-up." She removed the hair band from Maggie's head then began combing through Maggie's tangled mess.

Maggie took a sip. "Oh my," she exclaimed, "this is good."

"It's champagne with the new orange Red Bull and a floater of Peach Schnapps."

"It is *amazing*," Maggie said.

"A couple of those, you'll be brand new."

Tanya began working on Maggie's hair, expertly using a narrow paintbrush to apply the color to one section before moving on to the next section. Maggie's phone buzzed. She withdrew it from under her smock.

Britney: *Lunch?*
Maggie: *I'm so tired.*

> Britney: *Suck it up. Capital Grill?*
> Maggie: *Seriously...Tired*
> Britney: *Capital Grill?*
> Maggie: *Fine. What time?*
> Britney: *1*
> Maggie: *K*

"Ugh," Maggie said aloud. "Britney wants to do lunch."

"I love that girl," Tanya said. "We did a keratin treatment on her yesterday. It turned out amazing."

"Britney would look amazing if she was bald."

"Probably true."

"She wants to meet for lunch...but look at me?"

Tanya smiled. "Don't worry, we'll fix you up."

Maggie's phone buzzed again. She looked down and saw a text from Mike.

> Mike: *Hope you got home safe. Let me know when you want to try the gun range.*

Maggie couldn't help herself: she smiled but did not text back as Tanya moved her to the dryer. She sat for twenty minutes, giving her plenty of time to obsess over whether Mike was truly interested, looking for more information, or was just trying to be nice. She was more than grateful when Tanya handed her another glass of the magic juice. She was already feeling better.

When Maggie walked out of the Salon two hours later, she was indeed a new woman. Tanya had even applied some makeup, so she didn't even have to go home before she met Britney.

She had not quite driven one block when the August rains hit like a bucket of tacks, making it hard for Maggie to see two feet in front of her. She watched the thick black clouds chase her all the way to the restaurant, along with flashes of lightning with the rain. She pulled under the cover of the valet station, where she quickly released her keys to the valet and ran for the door. She had just reached the entrance when she saw Britney's SUV squeal into the parking lot, barely missing one curb. Then Britney bounced the vehicle over the other curb until she was safely parked—at an acute angle—under the valet cover. Thankfully, Maggie's car had already been moved. The young man dressed in black dress pants and a matching black vest opened Britney's door. She stumbled out happily, and the young man smiled wide as he walked her to the door where Maggie was waiting. The girls hugged briefly.

"I missed your face," Britney said.

"I just saw you yesterday," Maggie replied.

"Well, it was a long night." Britney smiled.

Maggie pulled the door open. She was hit with a rush of cool air. It was almost *too* cold; the warm wet air outside clung to her skin. She motioned Britney to go in.

Maggie followed Britney to the bar. They took a seat dead center, leaving an odd number of chairs at each side. Maggie always noticed these things; she had encouraged Britney several times to move over one seat, but now she kept silent. The only result would be an eye roll.

They were the only patrons at the bar, and the bartender was standing in front of them before they had a chance to settle more comfortably in their seats. He placed a bar napkin in front of each of them.

"Ladies," the handsome young man greeted them.

"Hi, Tyyyyyler!" Britney said, smiling sweetly.

"Heyyyy, Britney...you look amazing as usual."

Britney offered her cheek, and the bartender kissed it.

"Ice water, please," Britney said, "I need to hydrate."

"Me too," Maggie said. "And do you have any orange-flavored Red Bull?"

"Sorry, no," Tyler said, flashing a perfectly white straight smile.

This guy should be a model, not a bartender, Maggie thought.

"Okay, I'll just have a regular mimosa, but can you float it with Peach Schnapps?"

"Sure."

"I guess I'll have one of those too," Britney said.

Maggie turned to her friend. "Tanya made them for me at the salon, except with orange Red Bull."

Britney's eyes widened. "Now that sounds yummy."

"It was definitely better than coffee."

Britney stared at Maggie. "Your hair looks nice." She reached for a strand and flipped it.

"Thank you." Maggie nodded. "She always does such a good job."

"She really does," Britney said.

"Not to change the subject," Maggie said, pulling out her phone, "but you will not believe who has been texting me."

"Who?"

"Mike."

"Who is Mike?"

"The detective."

"Oh hell no. Maggie, don't go there." Britney was shaking her head.

"Why not?" Maggie smiled. "He's handsome and single."

"Seriously, Maggie, never trust a cop. He's probably married with three kids, beats his wife and kicks his dog."

"But…"

Maggie was just about to tell Britney about the plane ride, but she stopped herself, remembering the meeting with Britney's father.

"Well, I have a much better option for you," Britney said.

"Okay?"

"Remember I told you about the guy I met, Jay?"

"Yeah." Maggie didn't really remember Britney telling her about Jay, but it would be easier for her to just agree.

"Well, he has a friend."

Britney smiled. Tyler returned with the drinks, and Britney reached for her glass before Tyler could even put it down. Maggie picked up her glass and took a big long drink, emptying half of it.

"I'm sure his friend is too young for me," she said.

"You know I don't date men my age. They're both in their fifties but are in *great* shape."

"I don't know..." Maggie said.

"Here's to double dates." Britney held her glass up. "Cheers."

Maggie picked up her glass and downed the remaining half. Then she signaled to Tyler, who saw the empty glass and started fixing Maggie another one. "I'm not sure I can do a blind date at this point."

"Well, you better figure it out," Britney said, pointing to the door, "here they are."

"Oh shit."

Maggie watched two men walk toward the bar. One was blond with a short military-regulation haircut; the other was a dark-skinned man whose head was sheered almost bald. They *were* both handsome. Instantly, Maggie was glad she had not missed her hair appointment.

"Hey, Tyler," Britney said, "we're going to move over to that high-top." She pointed to the table she had in mind.

"I'll bring your drinks." Tyler was already coming from around the bar.

Britney and Maggie smiled as they met the guys at the table and sat across from each other. The blond with the military haircut leaned over and kissed Britney on the cheek. Maggie assumed this was Jay.

"I'm going to kill you," Maggie mouthed silently across the table to Britney.

"Chill out," Britney mouthed back with a huge smile.

"Have you ladies been waiting long?" Jay asked.

Britney smiled. "Not at all," she said.

Tyler set the drinks in front of the girls before turning to the guys. "What can I get you fellas?"

Jay pointed to the girls' drinks. "Whatever they're having."

"Me too," the other guy said, smiling at Maggie.

"So, this is Maggie," Britney said after Tyler had headed back to the bar. "She's my best friend."

"Hi, Maggie, I'm Jay"—he held out his hand—"and this is my best friend, Silas."

"Nice to meet you," Silas said, shaking Maggie's hand. His grip was firm and his skin not too soft. His warm brown eyes melted her as he made solid eye contact. Just like Britney said, both men were in great shape for their age.

Maggie could hardly take her eyes from Silas: he was still looking so directly in her eyes. She absolutely was impressed—and a little distracted—by the size of his arms. She had to make a concentrated effort not to stare; but he was *so* good looking… and his smile was entrancing. She was pretty sure he hailed from some exotic Latin country.

"Go ahead and touch them," he said without a hint of an accent.

"What?" Maggie felt her face turning red. She looked around, but Britney was already fully immersed in her own conversation with Jay. "Excuse me?"

He held up his arm and flexed. Without hesitation she reached out and put her hand on his bicep. It was rock-solid. She felt something stir in her, remembering her youth and the guys she had been attracted to…they all spent too much time in the gym. But in those days she was a tall thin girl with Farrah Fawcett hair.

"Very impressive," she said.

"I'm at the gym at five a.m. every day."

Of course you are.

"I can tell," she said aloud. The guy was definitely full of himself—but what the heck? She didn't have anything else going at this point, and Britney seemed to be fully engaged with Jay.

"What do you guys do for a living?" Maggie asked, smiling at Britney.

"Contractors," Jay said.

"Interesting," Britney said. She narrowed her eyes at Maggie. "What kind of contractors?"

"We build sea walls." Jay eyed Silas, who nodded his head in agreement.

"I bet that's big business around here," Maggie said.

"We mainly work in Miami but are down in the Keys at least once a month," Jay said.

"I love the Keys," Maggie said.

"We should all go down there," Silas said.

Britney spread her arms wide. "How about tomorrow?"

"Great idea, but we're busy tomorrow," Jay said.

Seeing the disappointment on Britney's face, Silas said, "It's a funeral."

"Oh no, I'm sorry." Maggie was relieved, truth be told. She didn't want to go to the Keys with guys she didn't even know.

"He had cancer," Jay explained, "so it's actually a relief he isn't suffering any longer."

"How old was he?" Britney asked. "Not that cancer discriminates."

"Fifty-seven," Jay said.

"Too young," added Silas.

Jay nodded. "His son just graduated high school."

A brief silence ensued. "Can we get four green tea shots?" Britney called to the bartender.

They waited quietly until the shots were placed in front of them.

"What's your friend's name?" Britney asked.

"Mark," Jay said.

They all lifted their shots.

"To Mark," Britney said.

"To Mark," the other three repeated.

"What do you ladies do?" Silas asked.

"I'm a contractor," Britney replied.

Both men turned to her, looking her up and down.

"What kind of contractor?" Jay asked.

"I'm a G-C," she said.

"You're a general contractor?" Silas raised his eyebrows in doubt.

Britney was used to this response, so she was prepared. She enjoyed the faces people made as they processed the contradiction. Their expressions usually changed from shock, to interest, to doubt, and finally to curiosity.

"That's a shocker," Jay said, "but very impressive."

"And you?" Silas asked Maggie.

"I'm a writer," Maggie said.

"Wow," Silas admired, "what do you write about?"

"Mostly technical stuff."

"Honestly? Sounds a little boring," Silas said.

"It is," Maggie said, smiling. "But I'm going to try writing some fiction."

Silas nodded. "That's cool," he said.

"Would you ladies be interested in dinner?" Jay asked after a moment.

Maggie looked down at her torn jeans and Chucks. "How about tomorrow?"

"The funeral is at two, how about we pick you girls up at seven o'clock?"

"How about PF Chang's," Britney suggested, "we can sit at the bar."

"Sounds good to me," Silas said.

"Perfect." Jay pulled a wad of cash from his pocket and waved at the bartender.

"I'll get mine," Maggie said.

Jay waved her away. "I got this."

Before Maggie could object, Britney had elbowed her into silence.

"Thank you," she squeaked out.

*

It was only 6:45 the next evening when Maggie's doorbell rang—and luckily she was ready. She opened the door to find Silas holding a small bouquet of flowers, obviously purchased at Publix.

"Come in," Maggie said.

Silas handed her the flowers. "Britney's idea."

"Of course." Maggie smiled tightly. "Please sit....Do you want a glass of wine or something?"

"I'll have a Bud Light if you have one."

"I have Corona Light."

"I'll take it."

"Lime?" Maggie asked. She walked into the kitchen and checked the vegetable drawer in the fridge.

"No thanks."

She was relieved. The only lime she had was so old, it looked like a chunk of petrified wood. She immediately threw it away and brought Silas the beer.

"Nice place," Silas said, looking around at Maggie's sparsely furnished home.

"Thanks, it's still a work in progress but definitely coming along." She paused, standing close beside him. "Are we meeting Jay and Britney at her house?"

"No, we're going to meet them there."

"Okay." She nodded, watching Silas down his entire beer in a matter of seconds. "Should we go?"

"Sure," Silas said. He was standing so close to Maggie she could feel the testosterone emanating from his skin. She breathed deep, taking it all in. She followed him to the door as if in a trance. Silas held it open and watched her walk through it.

"Are you going to lock it?" he asked, shaking her out of her fog.

"Oh, yeah."

She punched in the four-digit number: 1944, the year her mother was born.

"I hear you can't be too careful in this neighborhood." Silas laughed.

"Nope," she said, smiling in kind.

When they turned out of the screened-in porch, Maggie noticed the large black flatbed truck with giant chrome wheels parked in her driveway. The truck was lifted so high off the ground she wondered how she was going to gracefully climb into it, especially since the skirt she had chosen was on the shorter side, and the shoes were not the sensible type.

"Don't worry, I've got you." Silas must have recognized the panic on her face. He opened the door, and a sideboard step magically appeared from somewhere under the truck. "My lady…"

He held out his arm. Maggie stepped up onto the step and grabbed the handle just inside the door. Then she shifted her body until she was safely in the seat.

"Got it," she said.

Silas shut the door, and Maggie buckled her seat belt.

"This sure doesn't look like a contractor's truck," Maggie said when Silas slid in next to her.

"This is my toy," Silas explained proudly. "My work truck is a 2005 Chevy Duramax Diesel with three hundred and eleven thousand miles." He turned the key, causing a loud roar. Maggie jumped. She was sure the noise would irritate her neighbors. "Doesn't she sound great?" Silas asked. Maggie shook her head, lost in the whole experience….Not much later she and Silas had joined Britney and Jay at the bar at PF Chang's, where they promptly ordered drinks and dinner.

Because the four acquaintances were sitting in a row instead of facing each other, Maggie and Silas discussed Maggie's work in Seattle and her progress toward her new goals in fiction. Silas seemed genuinely interested. Maggie finally managed to take a breath, accepting this as a positive thing. Britney and Jay were also fully engaged; but they had already been out a few times, so they were even more at ease. Before Maggie knew it, their dinner was drawing to a close.

"Would you girls like to go over to Louie Bossi's for a nightcap?" Jay asked.

"You know I would," Britney said, "but I have an early morning flight and haven't even packed."

"Where are you going?" Jay asked.

"Bahamas," Britney said. "I need to walk a property and

bid a job."

"Why don't we all go?" Jay asked with a big smile. "My treat."

"I'm in," Silas said. "What airport?"

"Fort Lauderdale, six o'clock," Britney said. "Maggie?"

Maggie stared at her friend. She was stunned. The other three stood, waiting for her reply.

"I guess…" Maggie said softly.

"Well, okay, ladies, see you bright and early," Jay said.

When Maggie stood up, Silas slipped his arm around her shoulder. Together they walked out of the restaurant. He helped her into the truck—it was easier this time; but just before he shut the door, he rested his hand on her bare leg, sending shivers through her body.

"Wow," she said to herself, before he came around and climbed in.

During the short ride home, Silas told Maggie about growing up in the Dominican Republic and emigrating when he was twelve years old. He couldn't even speak English. Maggie was impressed: she could not detect an accent at all.

When they were finally parked in front of her house, Silas turned the engine off.

"I had a great evening," he said.

"I did too, thank you."

She unbuckled her seat belt, but before she got it off, he leaned over and kissed her. Hard.

"Wow," she said.

"Wow is right."

He kissed her again, and she responded, letting go of all inhibition; her senses returned only when a neighbor walked by. He held his dog's leash loosely in one hand and a small flashlight tightly in the other.

Silas sat back, breathing hard. "Neighborhood watch?"

"You're not kidding," Maggie said. "I don't even put my empty wine bottles in the recycle anymore after I saw one of my neighbors counting them."

Silas laughed as she opened the door. Then he quickly got out and ran around the truck in time to help her down.

"Would you like me to come in?" he asked.

"Um, well," she said. "But if we're going to the Bahamas tomorrow, I really have to pack."

"I'm really looking forward to tomorrow, Maggie," Silas said in a low voice.

Maggie swallowed hard. "Me too."

"Goodnight, Silas." Maggie shut the door. She leaned against it until she heard Silas's truck start up and drive away.

Maggie's cell rang, bringing her out of her fog. She looked at the screen, hoping it was Silas, but it was Britney.

"Do you like him?" Britney asked.

"Oh yeah," Maggie said.

"This is going to be so fun."

"I'm a little nervous that we don't even know these guys and we're going to another country. What if they kidnap us?"

"Just go with it. It's only a couple days, not a lifetime commitment. They're not kidnappers."

"I do really like him, but…" Maggie started.

"You'll be fine. Actually, you'll be better than fine, you're probably going to get laid."

"Oh my God, girl, good night."

Maggie pushed the disconnected the call, not even letting Britney say goodnight.

CHAPTER 17

Hurricane

"This machine isn't working," Maggie said as she attempted to check in at a Spirit Airlines kiosk.

"Mine worked," Britney said, pulling her ticket and receipt from the dispenser.

"Oh wow, there are the guys," Maggie said. "What the hell are we doing?"

Britney smiled encouragingly at Maggie. "Chill, mama. This is going to be fun."

"Whatever, you say Britney, I'm trusting you."

The men approached the two women.

"Hey guys," Britney said, "ready for some fun?"

Jay embraced her. Silas embraced Maggie.

"You girls checked in?" Jay asked.

"I am, but Maggie is having an issue."

"I'll go up to the counter and see what I can do," Maggie said. "You guys go ahead."

"I'll go with you," Silas said.

Maggie pulled her suitcase toward the counter. She noticed Silas had both a suitcase and a large duffle bag with him.

"That's a lot of luggage for a weekend," Maggie said.

"This bag just has shoes." Silas held up the duffle. Maggie considered how many pairs of shoes she had brought: one. And she was wearing them. Maybe she should have brought at least one more pair?

The Spirit agent took Maggie's license and asked for her passport. She handed him her passport card; she had not been able to find her passport.

"I need your actual passport," the agent said.

"That's all I got," she answered. "It says I can use it for the Bahamas on the back."

"It actually says by land or sea." The agent pointed to the small print. "You have to have a real passport to fly."

"You have to be kidding," Maggie said, defeated.

"No, sorry," the agent replied. "But there are two more flights that go out today and three more tomorrow; so if you find your passport, we can likely get you on one of those."

"I just have no idea where it could be…." Maggie shook her head.

"There's a same day passport office in Miami. If you get there by noon, you might be able to make the five o'clock flight," the agent said.

"Really?" Maggie said. "Thank you."

She turned to Silas. "You guys go, I'll try to get there this afternoon."

"How about we let Jay and Britney go and I'll come to Miami with you?"

"Seriously," Maggie replied, "you don't need to do that. I don't want to ruin your vacation."

"The only reason I agreed to go was to get to know you better," Silas told her candidly. He put his hand on her shoulder. "Now we just have more one-on-one time; so let's go tell those two."

Britney and Jay agreed to go ahead, saying they would meet Silas and Maggie later at the bar at the SLS Baha Mar.

"We can take my car, I parked in valet," Maggie said. They had left the ticketing area and were approaching the parking garages.

Silas looked surprised. "You parked in valet at the airport?"

"Britney has a pass, so it doesn't really cost anything except a tip."

"Well, I'll get that," Silas said. He dug in his pocket then pulled out a huge wad of cash. He peeled back a few hundreds until he reached a twenty. "Do you think this is good?"

Maggie raised an eyebrow. "Very generous," she said.

When the valet handed her the keys, she turned to Silas and held them out to him "Would you mind driving? I don't know my way around Miami."

Silas nodded. "Not a problem." They climbed into the car. "Can you bring up the map to the place?"

"Sure…Siri says head south."

Silas nodded then drove out of the parking area and exited the airport. Maggie relaxed once he merged onto the highway.

"I am sure sorry about this," she said. "I should have paid more attention."

"Aw, relax, no problem," Silas told her reassuringly. "We'll get there eventually, and if we don't we can go out to a nice dinner here tonight."

Maggie smiled. "You're sweet."

"Thank you, I try," he said, placing his hand on her bare leg.

"What's it like in the Dominican Republic?"

Silas scoffed. "It's a shithole."

"I wish I knew more Spanish…" Maggie said.

He shifted in the driver's seat. "Not to change the subject, but tell me about this dead guy? Britney was telling Jay what you girls are up to. Sounds interesting."

"It's actually kind of a crazy story, but we have a few suspects."

"What do you mean 'we' have suspects?"

"Well, it's just for fun. Britney, Alex, and I are seriously investigating the murder."

Silas shook his head. "That doesn't sound very smart."

Maggie laughed. "We live in a country club, what could happen behind the gates?"

"I don't know, the killer might kill you too?"

"Honestly, I think it was just a terrible accident. Marco and Rodney were probably just fooling around, and Rodney was so drunk he pulled the trigger, shot Marco in the chest, and went to sleep."

"That sounds pretty unlikely," Silas said, "No matter how drunk you are, I think you might realize that you just shot someone with a crossbow."

Maggie considered. Then she said, "I'll bet if the cops tested Rodney they might have found Oxy in his system."

"I'm sure they tested his blood for everything," Silas said. "Do you know if he's been cleared?"

"I don't know." She shook her head. "I tried to get it out of the detective, but he wouldn't tell me anything."

"You mind?"

Silas didn't wait for Maggie's answer, he simply plugged his phone into Maggie's car radio and pushed a few buttons. The screen flashed a couple of times: several rows of random letters and numbers flashed across it so fast Maggie barely had time to notice. Then the name Ana Vidovic settled in the middle of the screen and the most elegant, stunning music surrounded her.

Maggie looked at Silas. "Is that a woman playing the guitar?"

"Yes, isn't she incredible?"

"I've never heard anything like it…"

"There's something about the Spanish guitar…It's like listening to a full orchestra." Silas's face seemed to soften as he talked. "Very relaxing…."

"Do you play an instrument?" Maggie asked.

"I play the bongos," he said proudly, "but my preference is dancing. Do you dance salsa?"

Maggie laughed out loud. "Nope. I don't dance."

"I bet you would be a great dancer, with those hips," he said.

Maggie decided not to take offense. Instead she changed the subject.

"We have another ten miles to go," she said, looking at the map on her phone.

"It's getting close to lunch," Silas said. "Why don't you give the passport place a call and ask if they're open during lunch. If not we can stop, I know of a great Cuban place not too far from here."

Maggie called the instant passport shop the agent had recommended. Surprisingly an actual person answered, not a machine. Maggie explained the situation then fell silent for a few minutes as she listened to the person on the other end of the line and nodded her head as if the person could see her. She listened a little longer then, finally, shook her head.

"Well, that's not good news," she said as she hung up her phone.

"Uh oh, what?"

"No way I'm getting a passport today. Even if I do all the paperwork, the fastest I can have it is Monday morning."

"That sucks," Silas said. He fell silent for a moment. "You have no idea where yours is?"

"I looked everywhere. I know I have it, I just used it a few months ago." She shook her head, admonishing herself. "I remember putting it somewhere safe, maybe too safe."

"Let's go back to your house and take a look." Silas shrugged. "If we don't find it, no biggy."

"Okay, let's go," Maggie said, raising her hand and twirling her finger in the air.

Silas took the next exit then crossed the overpass. He got back onto I-95, heading north.

Maggie was lost in thought, trying to remember where she had put her passport. When they came to the turn signal for the country club, she fished her driver's license out of her pocketbook to hand to the gate guard. Silas had already rolled his window down. Maggie saw that the guard was a young Hispanic man she had noticed all the time driving through the community in one of the security trucks.

"Hey, man." Silas took the license from Maggie's hand and held it out to the guard.

"Hey, how's it going?" The young man took barely a glance at the license then pushed the button for the gate. "Take it easy."

Silas drove through the gate. "Do you know that guy?" Maggie asked.

Silas smiled. "How would I know him?"

"I don't know…it's like you had a thing."

"A thing, Maggie?" He looked at her sideways with a smirk on his face. "I have no idea what you're talking about."

"How—"

Maggie stopped herself from asking the rest of her question, which had just occurred to her. *How did you get in the other night to pick me up?* She had never called him in. And that led to the next question: how had he known where she lived? Britney must have told him, she concluded.

"How what?" Silas asked.

"How long do we have?" Maggie answered calmly.

"As much time as we need, babe."

Silas winked at her and smiled. Maggie smiled back.

Once they reached her house Maggie had Silas pull around to the garage. They entered the house together, through the garage door. Silas followed her into the wide-open space comprising her living room, dining room, and home office. She pulled open a few file cabinet doors and pointed at her desk.

"I've looked through all of this but it could use a fresh set of eyes. I'll go look in my bedroom."

"If you need any help in there…" Silas suggested playfully.

"I'm good for now," she replied, but her mind said *If you only knew….*

Maggie started opening drawers and checking jewelry boxes. She pulled out the small safe from the closet; it wasn't even locked. Then she emptied the contents onto her bed. Everything was actually pretty well organized, the envelopes were clearly marked. There was even an envelope marked Passports—but when she opened it she found they were all old or expired. The current passport wasn't there.

She took the safe back to the closet and began to dig through her old handbags. She was about to give up when she noticed a wallet on one of the shelves. She picked it up. Underneath it lay an old fanny pack. She pulled the fanny pack off the shelf, and sure enough, it held a few credit cards, an old driver's license—and her passport. She dropped everything and ran into the living room. Silas was methodically searching through her files.

"I found it!" She held the passport up to show Silas. "Let's go!"

"Well, let's go then," he said. He began putting everything back in the cabinets.

"Forget that!" Maggie insisted. "If we get back to the airport, we can be there by two."

When they closed the door to the house, Silas punched in the code. Maggie watched in surprise.

*

The flight was short and uneventful. Maggie was simply relieved she hadn't ruined the entire trip. She was impressed how Silas had taken it all in stride.

As soon as they walked into the hotel, they spotted the bar. Jay and Britney were sitting there, speaking to a man in a suit.

"You made it!" Britney leaped out of her seat and embraced Maggie. "I honestly didn't think you were going to make it!"

Maggie laughed, shaking her head. "Honestly, I didn't either, but we're here."

"This is Franz, he's the GM here." Britney turned to the tall-suited gentleman whom she and Jay had been speaking to. "This is my best friend, Maggie."

Franz nodded to Maggie and bowed slightly. "If you ladies need anything, let me know. I made reservations for seven tonight at the steak house, my treat."

"Thank you, Franz, you're the best," Britney said.

"I'm just glad you're going to take on our little project," Franz replied.

"I'm looking forward to it." Britney smiled.

Franz turned to Maggie. "Nice to meet you." Then he waved to the guys and walked away.

Maggie looked at Britney, surprised. "You took the job?"

"Hell yeah, I took the job. It's a half-million-dollar project!"

"That's a 'small' project?"

Britney gazed purposefully at Maggie. "You need a drink, my friend…you have got some catching up to do."

Maggie looked over where the guys stood. Both had a beer in their hands.

Britney motioned to the bartender. "What are you going to have—wine, mimosa, what?"

"What's your specialty tonight?" Maggie asked.

"Hurricane," the bartender pushed a table tent toward her with the picture of a tall pink concoction garnished with an orange slice and a cherry .

"That sounds about right, I'll have one of those," Maggie said.

The bartender turned to Britney.

"Better make that two," she said. She turned back to Maggie. "I honestly thought you were not going to make it."

"I honestly didn't think I would, but it must have been meant to be." Then Maggie remembered: "Did you happen to call Silas in the gate last night?"

"No." Britney shook her head. "Why?"

"We'll talk later." Silas moved next to her, setting his arm around Maggie's waist, pulling her close. The good, strong physical contact made Maggie forget about everything, except how good Silas made her feel.

*

When the two couples walked into Katsuya, they were

greeted by Franz, who promptly walked them to a table he had reserved for them. As soon as they settled into their seats, a man wearing a black vest over a simple white dress shirt appeared directly behind Franz. Franz nodded to the four friends. "I leave you now in the very capable hands of our sommelier, Jeff Delaney," he said. Then he moved aside, bowed slightly, and disappeared.

"Good evening," the sommelier said, addressing them formally. "As Franz said, I am pleased to be at your service this evening, and I would like to start the evening with a very special champagne"—he displayed the bottle to them—"chosen just for you by our chef." Jeff expertly popped the cork on the bottle. Four crystal glasses appeared, carried on a small tray by a gentleman wearing attire similar to Jeff's.

"I will give you a few minutes to relax then return with recommendations once you have chosen your meal." He moved aside, letting the second gentleman step to the table.

"Good evening," he said, passing out menus. "My name is Jesus Martinez, and I will have the pleasure of serving you this evening." He smiled. As he handed Silas his menu they nodded to each other as though acknowledging some common Latino brotherhood. "May I offer a recommendation this evening?"

"Please," Britney spoke up.

"For starters, the chef recommends the king crab tempura and the yellowtail with jalapeño. For the main course, we have a special premium A-4 Japanese Wagyu beef, grilled medium well and garnished with fresh wasabi. Tonight we also have a fresh salmon grilled on a cedar plank and garnished with tomato, caper, and sansho peppercorn sauce. For dessert you must try the chocolate lava cake, it is to die for. Of course, everything on our menu is fresh and delicious."

"We'll take one of each of the appetizers, and four salads," Britney said. "And I'll take the steak."

"Madam?" Jesus turned to Maggie.

"I'll have the salmon."

"Sir?" He turned to Silas.

"Quiero el filete, por favor."

"Lo tengo," the waiter replied, nodding at Silas then turning to Jay. "Sir?"

"I'll also have the steak, but I'd like it well done."

"Very good. Anything else I can get you right now?"

"I think we're good," Jay said.

As soon as the waiter disappeared, Britney raised her glass. "Cheers."

"Cheers," the other three repeated.

As soon as the salads were set down in front of them, Jeff, the sommelier, returned.

"Based on your choices, I would recommend a nice Domaine du Pegau Chateauneuf-du-Pape Cuvee Reserve 2015, it is from the Côtes du Rhône region. It is a great pairing for the steak; and for the salmon, I would suggest a California wine, Williams Selyem Russian River Valley Pinot Noir 2017."

"Well, I'm not much of a wine drinker," Silas said, "so can I get a Bud Light?"

"Of course, sir."

"I'll also take a Bud Light," Jay said.

"I think we'll both take the wine," Britney said. Maggie nodded her head.

As soon as Jeff had left the table, Britney stood up. "Maggie?"

Maggie took the not so subtle hint. "Excuse us," she said, joining her friend. She followed Britney out of the restaurant and back into the hotel. They paused for a moment to take a picture next to the large portrait of a monkey near the lobby; then they headed into the bathroom.

"These guys are fun," Britney said, looking in the mirror while adding some lip gloss. Maggie took the opportunity to use the toilet; she didn't answer until she was at the sink washing her hands. "The only thing I find odd is that Silas seems like he knows everyone." She carefully fingered some stray hairs into place. "He even acted like he knew the gate guard at the club. "

"I think he's just one of those people who instantly

connects with others," Britney responded. "Kind of like you, actually. I don't think you've ever met a stranger."

As soon as they were seated at the table again, Jeff was pouring their wine, and the guys were already ordering another beer.

"Why is it..." Jay started.

"Don't," Britney interrupted.

Jay gave her a look. "I was just going to ask..."

"We go together so we can talk about you," she said. They all chuckled.

The conversation soon shifted to Marco and his murder.

"Did you know Marco?" Jay asked Maggie.

"I guess as much as you could know Marco," Maggie said.

"Did you give him money too?" Jay asked.

Jay's question caused Maggie to swallow hard. She was obviously uncomfortable with the conversation. Clearly, Jay had already had this conversation with Britney, and she had told him about the money.

"I think he owed a lot of people money," Maggie said softly, not admitting anything.

"I think Alexandra lost the most," Britney said.

"Why's that?" Jay asked.

"They made the cardinal mistake," Maggie said.

Jay looked at her. "What was that?"

"Mixing business with pleasure. She really did like him. I think he actually liked her too, but he was so full of himself he couldn't see them as a couple."

This time Silas asked: "Why's that?"

"Alex thinks it was her age. He couldn't get past it."

"She *is* a beautiful classy woman," Silas said.

Maggie stared at him. "Do you know Alex...?"

"No, but the way you two talk about her, I'm sure she is," Silas said.

"She really is," Britney replied, "and she really liked him."

By the end of the night, Maggie had consumed the full bottle of wine at dinner, and after a few more after-dinner drinks, she was especially glad that she had taken extra time with a razor before the trip. Silas proved to be especially attentive. It had been over three years since Maggie had spent a night with a man, and the fun of the day just continued through the night....

*

Maggie woke in a fog, realizing the shower was running in her bathroom. The personification of her joyous night walked in with a towel wrapped around his midsection. Maggie blinked a few times to make sure what she was seeing was real. This guy had some abs...or pecks....or whatever chest muscles were called. She pulled the covers closer to hide her jelly belly, muffin-top body.

Silas smiled wide. "Good morning, beautiful."

"Good morning," Maggie replied.

"Ready for breakfast?"

"Uh, well I need a few minutes to get ready...."

"I'll tell you what, I'll go find my room and get dressed," Silas said. "I'll meet you at that little restaurant right off the lobby in half an hour." He picked his clothes off the floor and walked out the door, still wearing just a towel.

"Sure, sounds good," Maggie said to the already closed door.

She climbed out of the bed but kept the sheet wrapped around her even though she was alone in the room. *"What the hell am I doing?"* she said to herself. *"Just go with it,"* she answered herself. *"Just go with it."*

Silas was already sitting at a table outside when Maggie came down. He saw her and stood up to pull out a chair.

"Sorry I took so long."

"You're right on time."

Silas motioned the server, who placed a cup of coffee in front of Maggie. Maggie eyed him as she took the cup in both hands and took a sip. "How did you know I liked coffee?"

"You look like a coffee drinker," Silas answered, smiling.

The server reappeared, ready to take the order. Silas ordered an egg white vegetable omelet, no cheese, and sliced tomatoes instead of hash browns. Maggie ordered two eggs over easy, hash browns, and white toast. She wanted to ask if the restaurant had a little sausage gravy the chef could put on the hash browns, but she decided not to. Instead, she decided to hire a personal trainer when she got home.

CHAPTER 18

Mojito

All three ladies sat in the back of the Uber. Maggie rested her head against the window, Britney was texting on her phone, and Alexandra was fixing her lipstick, holding a small mirror.

"I have something to tell you guys," Maggie said. She lifted her head and faced the others.

"What is it, sweetie?" Alexandra asked. She smacked her lips then blotted them with a tissue she had tucked in her sleeve. Britney pushed a few more buttons before dropping her phone into her lap.

"Marco conned me for ten thousand dollars but I didn't tell the detective."

"What?" Alex asked in a low tone. "Why?"

"Why what? Why did he take my money?"

"Why did you *loan* him the money?"

Maggie sighed softly. "I don't know how it happened, exactly. He just came over to look at the wall between my bathroom and the atrium I had turned into my office. There's a big window he said could be turned into a fish tank. He said he knew someone who could do it. I mean, can you imagine some jellyfish floating around? It would have been *so* cool."

"Okay...but how did the money come up?" Alex again

asked.

"We were sitting on the couch…I had poured us of each a glass of wine. We were talking about ideas for the place. It was so '80s but had character. He actually had a great eye. He suggested that I take the wall down between the kitchen and living room—like he had. I said I was conflicted with the idea. I've seen it done both ways, and I was leaning toward keeping the wall. The next thing you know he was telling me about his sister Angie and all her problems in her marriage. He said that he was helping her out and he could barely afford his club dues this month. He said he had a contract that he had been working for two years finally coming through."

"Rehab facilities?" Britney asked.

"Yes, exactly," Maggie said.

"Oh Lord." Alex rolled her eyes.

"He said he would pay me back and get me the fish tank at his cost."

"And you gave him the money?" Alex asked.

"Ugh, I didn't want to," Maggie admitted. "I knew it wasn't the smartest decision I ever made…but he said Angie was in real trouble and her husband was abusive. He said he was paying for her attorney. He also said he was supporting his mother in New York. I'm a sucker for a sad story."

"Well, the story of his sister and mom are both true," Alex said. "I checked it out."

"Did you give him money too?" Britney asked.

"Yes and no," Alex said. "We were actually business partners."

"Business partners?" both Maggie and Britney asked.

"Oh my God, Alexandra, you didn't tell us," Britney said.

"I never mix business and personal relationships," she said.

"Except…" Britney said.

"It was purely by accident it came up at all. Marco and I had gone to dinner one night, and somehow the conversation always seemed to turn out to be business focused. He was always asking for business advice.

I somehow thought it was his way of getting close. You know, a way to break the ice—and one thing for sure was I have business experience. Marco actually was interested, he absorbed everything I had to say. Sometimes I would get two or three calls a day where he would go through a list of questions."

"We both know you liked him, Alex, more than a friend," Britney said.

"Was it really obvious?"

"Yes, but you shouldn't feel ashamed," Maggie said. "He was a good-looking guy with a silver tongue."

"I admit it was flattering, this young good-looking man turning to me for advice. One night we were having dinner at Mr. Chang's, and I was telling him about a deal I just landed in Brazil. Since he was from there, I thought he would find it interesting…but when I mentioned Avianca Brazil, he started shaking his head.

It was a big deal for our small company, Avianca is the fourth-largest airline in Brazil. I had just shipped more than a million dollars' worth of electronics, which was already in transit. His face twisted up like something was wrong, and he made a call. When he hung up, he told me that the airline was just about to file for bankruptcy.

"If Avianca took physical possession of the material, it would become a part of their assets and we might never get paid—or if we did, it would be for pennies on the dollar. Marco was a smart guy, and since my company was the legal owner until delivery was made, we could intercept the delivery, take possession, and return the shipment. Marco said he had friends who could delay the delivery until we got there, but we needed to leave tomorrow.

"I made some calls and lined up transportation for the next day. I was just so thankful for Marco at that point."

Britney eyed Alex uncertainly. "Are you sure that it was all true? How would he know about the airline going bankrupt?"

"I didn't know for sure, but I decided to go with my gut and trust him. That big of a loss could seriously cripple my company. So we made plans to go to Brazil and get my material before it was delivered. I made arrangements for a plane leaving out of Boca the next morning.

"As soon as I stepped onto the plane I saw Marco comfortably sitting in one of the oversized leather seats; he already had a drink in hand. He was wearing a white linen suit which looked *so* Miami Vice, but with his Italian complexion and white smile, I just kind of melted into my seat. He was drinking some kind of Brazilian local drink called a caipirinha. I took a sip, but it was too sweet, so I just ordered a mojito."

"I *love* mojito's," Britney said.

"Keep going," Maggie said. "I just can't believe you never told us about this."

"When we landed in São Paulo, we checked into Hotel Emiliano and waited for a phone call. The meeting was scheduled for ten a.m. the next day, so we settled in for the evening, had a nice dinner and an amazing bottle of wine, maybe two bottles, followed by a Disaronno. I found myself caught up in the whole evening, it was romantic…Marco was so incredibly interesting…highly educated, and obviously very handsome. I was feeling light-headed by the time we went to our rooms."

"What?" Britney exploded. "I don't believe you. You're telling us nothing happened?"

"I didn't say that. As soon as I closed the door there was a tap—and Marco came in. I'm not saying how long he stayed, but that man was magic."

Maggie held up both hands. "No more," she said.

"What are you talking about?" Britney objected. "*I* would like to hear some juicy stuff…"

"Well, let's just say…*wow*! It had been a long dry spell so…you know."

"Oh my god!" Maggie exclaimed.

"Anyway, the next day we met a guy and the truck driver, I handed them each an envelope with, let's say, a lot of cash. No matter, it saved me from much bigger losses. Then Marco took me to the business district and to a top floor office building that was one big space with no individual offices but a few desks scattered throughout. In the center of the space was a large table set up with a scale model of a beautiful resort.

Marco was mostly speaking Portuguese to the others but explained to me that this was an E-B-5 project and this was the investment firm set up to offer the investors green cards. He explained that for a minimum investment of five hundred thousand dollars, the investor received a green card and basically a fast track to citizenship.

It's a government program designed to stimulate employment in the construction industry. The investor has to invest the money for five years and gets no interest on the investment."

Maggie looked at Britney for any sign of a reaction but there was none. Maggie felt her face flush but wasn't going to expose Britney's tie to the scheme.

"So, he sat me down at his desk and told me that he had several Brazilian investors ready to invest as soon as the project was approved. The problem was it cost over one hundred thousand dollars to even get the permits submitted."

"You didn't," Britney said.

Alexandra nodded. "I was still under his spell from the night before. Plus he said it would be less than six months to get the money back plus interest. He had just saved me ten times that, so I believed him."

"How long ago was that, Alex?" Maggie asked.

"More than two years. He always had an excuse not to pay me back."

"Did you get anything on paper?" Britney asked.

Alexandra just shook her head no. "For such a smart woman, I really can't understand my lack of judgment," she acknowledged. "And now I'll never get my money back."

Maggie shook her head. "I don't think you should be beating yourself up now…"

"You're the smartest woman I know," Britney chimed in, "and your heart is your biggest asset. Does a hundred thousand dollars really make a difference to your life?"

"Well, yes," Alex said. "It does."

"Really?"

"Okay, no. But I remember a time when I was a young woman who couldn't put five dollars of gas in her car."

"We can hardly live in the past, and we all need to move forward from here." Britney nodded firmly. "There's no way to retaliate. Someone took out the trash for us."

Maggie smiled wide. "Did you really just say that?"

"I did."

Maggie laughed. Then she said, "I'm hungry."

The car stopped in front of Capital Grill. And the three women got out and headed for the door, which was already being held open by one of the handsome young valet crew.

They took seats at the high-top nearest the bar. It was a light crowd for happy hour, but the snowbirds were still up north. The girls still had a month or two to enjoy the lighter traffic and open tables.

A server walked by with two bowls of the restaurant's French onion soup.

"I need some of that," Maggie said.

"This place has *the* best French onion soup I have ever had in my life," Alex said.

"I just need a drink," Britney replied.

And at that exact moment, Tyler, the bartender, appeared at Britney's side.

"What do you beautiful girls want to drink?" Tyler said, setting down three glasses of water.

"Mojito," Britney said.

"Make that two," Alex said.

Maggie held up three fingers.

"You got it!"

All three ladies watched Tyler walk away until he disappeared behind the bar.

"I went out with him," Alex said.

"Marco?" Maggie asked.

"No." Alex smiled. "Tyler, the bartender."

"What?" Britney returned Alex's smile. "There's so much we just don't know about you, woman."

"How old is he?" Maggie asked.

"Old enough," Alex said, sipping her water. "Does it really matter?"

"I'm so proud of you," Britney said.

"Age is just a number, girls. I was married faithfully for thirty-five years to the love of my life—but he's gone. I finally realized that I'm not going to be here forever. I'm not wasting any good years I still have."

"You go girl," Maggie said.

As soon as Tyler set the drinks in front of the girls, they unwrapped the straws and began to sip.

"I hate these stupid paper straws," Maggie said.

Alex agreed. "They melt too fast."

Britney reached into her bag, pulled out a light blue pouch. "Look at this." She slipped out a glass straw with a metal Tiffany's logo and plunked it into her drink.

"Nice," Maggie said, "but what if it breaks?"

"Then you can't use it," Britney said. "I actually invented these things but waited too long to market it. Now they're *everywhere*."

"I think it's a fad…what's the big deal about straws?" Maggie said.

"Turtles," Britney said.

"What about the tops of water bottles or plastic sandwich bags?"

"I suppose those are problems too—but I'm doing my part right here," Britney said, holding up the glass straw.

"What about you, Britney? Now that we both confessed," Alex said.

"Do I have to?"

"Of course you do," Alex said. "It can't be worse than my

story."

Britney sighed then dove right in: "So, I had just gotten home from an appointment in Miami, I barely had time to change my clothes, and there was a knock at the door. I looked at the security cameras and saw it was Marco. It actually caught me off guard, but I answered the door.

He said he needed to talk to me about something important. I told him I had just gotten home and could we meet up at the club in an hour. He insisted it was urgent and just came in.

"He picked up my dog and sat on the couch like he belonged there. I reluctantly sat too, facing him, and he starts telling me how he can't trust anyone, how I was one of the only women he respects, blah blah blah."

Alex nodded. "Seriously," she said, "those are the exact words he used on me."

"Anyway, he goes on and on until finally I say, 'Marco, what do you want?'

"He smiled and explained he needed to use my contractor license for a small project he was bidding on. It was a private school in Fort Lauderdale. He said it was short term and he would have it wrapped up in a month."

"What does he know about contracting?" Maggie asked.

"I think we would be surprised at all the things he has a hand in," Alex replied.

Britney continued: "Well, I said no, but somehow he just kept on and on until I finally gave in."

"I don't believe you," Maggie said. "No way you folded that easy."

"I agree." Alex nodded.

"Okay…well…he had some information on a project I was working on. Actually. Alex, it's the same project you invested in."

"Oh no," Alex said.

"You cannot say *anything* to *anybody*," Britney said.

"Of course," Alex said. Maggie already knew the situation so she sat silent as Britney finished recounting it to Alex. Then she turned to Maggie. "Remember I told you about my friend Brandon who was in jail?"

"Yes," Maggie said.

"Marco knew him...*and* he knew my connection to the Boca Palms Resort project," Britney said. "He basically told me that if I didn't let him use my license, he would expose the connection. I told him to F-off but he just laughed and gave me twenty-four hours. I called my dad, and I ended up letting him use the license."

"Why?" Maggie asked.

"My dad said he would make sure nothing happened with my license. He has a contact at the county's building department who could change the number on any permits submitted under my company name."

"I love it," Alex said.

"Did he use it?"

"I don't know what he used it for, but he never filed for any permits at the county, thank god. But he did get ten thousand dollars out of me."

"Of course he did," Alex said. "That's why we're drinking."

Maggie was confused. She wondered whether Britney remembered she was at the meeting with her at the cigar bar... Which version of her story was the truth?

"When I first moved here," Maggie said, "Marco was one of the first people I met. He was really nice to me, and he seemed to have a big heart. When I needed help getting rid of all the old furniture that came with my house, he offered to haul it all away. It was nice stuff, just not my style. In fact, I'm sure it was much more expensive than what I replaced it with. He knew of some Guatemalan families who would love to have it, so he sent a couple guys over and they hauled it all away."

"He had his moments," Alex said, nodding.

"He actually helped me find a pool guy, landscaper, and a housekeeper," Maggie acknowledged.

"Ooohh, the housekeeper," Britney said. "Maybe *she's* our killer?"

"She's been out of the country," Maggie said, "her daughter just had a baby."

"I think Jamaica or maybe New York," Alex said.

"Seriously? There *is* a big difference," Britney said. "New York is just a few hours away."

"I know she's from Jamaica and some family is in New York. I have a hard time understanding her accent. That's why I take a book up to the club while she's cleaning my house. Sometimes she just wants to chat, and those bathrooms don't clean themselves."

"Ha ha ha," Alex said, "I do the same thing."

"I just go to work," Britney said.

"Do you girls want to hear my Marco story?" Maggie asked the two women who were now staring at her.

"Of course," Alex said raising an eyebrow.

"Well, Marco invited me to dinner at City Fish."

"And you went?" Alex asked.

"Yeah, he caught me off guard and Marco is hard to say no to. He kind of didn't ask but told me we were going."

"*Definitely* Marco's style," Alex said.

"So, we get to City Fish and sit at one of the booths in the bar. I ordered a wine and had just opened the happy hour menu, and he ordered for both of us. I have to say that's one thing I do *not* appreciate. I *can* order my own food. The server puts a basket of bread in front of us and, get this, he actually butters a piece and sits it on my plate."

"Some girls like that," Britney said.

"Not this girl," Maggie said. "What am I, three?"

"I drank my whole glass of wine and he ordered me another before the food even got there." Maggie shook her head as she continued her story.

"He was trying to get you drunk," Britney said.

"I drank three glasses, but he wasn't dealing with an amateur. My wits were full intact. That is until we were back in my living room. He was telling me how he had a deal he was working on and it was in its final stages. He said I was one of the few people he could trust and he was thankful we had become such close friends. At that point, I was thinking he must not have *any* friends, because honestly, we hadn't really ever had any in-depth conversations. During the previous week, he would text me and say stuff like, *What's up, good-looking?* or *How's your day so far, beautiful?*

Honestly, I thought it a lame attempt at flirting. Now I see it was grooming me for this very evening. At this point I was ready to get into my comfy pajamas, but he seemed to be oblivious and took a seat on the couch. He starts asking me personal questions about my family, my career…you know, that kind of stuff.

I kept my answers short and kept yawning so he would get the hint. Finally, it came out, he wanted to 'borrow' twenty-five thousand dollars for a few weeks, possibly a month. I told him I didn't have that kind of money. He said, how about a credit card? I told him I was right in the middle of remodeling, and I didn't have much available balance.

He says, 'How much is that?' I couldn't think fast enough and said ten thousand dollars. 'Perfect,' he said. He actually pulled out his cell phone, attached some kind of swiper thing, and held out his hand. Stupid me, I dug out my wallet and handed him the card. Thank God, I didn't tell him the truth. I don't carry a balance on that card, and I've got all kinds of credit."

"How long ago was that?" Alex asked.

"A year."

"Did you get any of it back?" Britney asked.

"Did either of you?"

"What a shithead," Britney said.

"What I don't understand is where did all the money go?" Alex asked. "He drove a five-year-old Cadillac and didn't have anything fancy. He bought his suits at Men's Warehouse."

"Maybe he had a gambling problem?" Maggie suggested.

"Nah," Britney said. "I think we would know that…but I can ask my dad."

"I think he might be stashing it in Brazil," Alex said.

"But why?" Britney asked.

Maggie agreed. "Who would want to live there?" she said.

"It's not too bad *if* you have money," Alex replied. "Plus he grew up there."

"If he was doing something illegal, wouldn't he have been extradited?" Maggie asked.

"Brazil does not extradite their citizens," Alex said. "He had a Brazilian passport. Since he was born there, he has dual citizenship. I think the worse that could happen would be they might have revoked his American passport."

"Interesting," Britney said.

"We should take a trip to Brazil," Maggie said, "check it out."

"I don't think so." Alex shook her head. "It's not Kansas, Dorothy."

A silence fell over the table. Maggie thought for a moment; then she pulled from her purse the report Rodney had produced for her of the cars entering the gates of the country club the night of the murder. "I have to show you this. Look who came in twice the night Marco died."

Maggie moved her drink aside and set the paper in the middle of the table. She put her finger on a name.

"Marco?" Britney said, confused.

"Not Marco. Angie. The Toyota is her car…but since Marco is the member, it's listed under his name. Anyway, look at the time. She came in at 12:15 a.m. and then again at 4:30."

"Unbelievable. I wonder if the police ever got this log?" Alex asked.

"I'm sure they have it," Britney said, "but I wonder why she hasn't been arrested. It's obvious she killed him…but how did she think she could get away with it?"

"It's not obvious, maybe someone else was driving her car," Maggie said.

"Like who?" Britney asked.

Alex said, "Preston, her ex. Maybe he had a set of keys."

"Now we have a real suspect," Maggie said.

Alex nodded. "Let's call Angie."

"I'll do it." Maggie pulled out her phone to text Rodney.

> Maggie: *Hey do you have Angie's number?*
> Rodney: *Hey? No hello...how are you...how is it going?*
> Maggie: *Hello Rodney, how is it going?*
> Rodney: *Thanks for asking. I'm doing great. Are you free for lunch tomorrow?*
> Maggie: *Seriously?*
> Rodney: *I just sent Angie's contact info and yeah seriously. There is a wine tasting event Friday at the club. Interested?*
> Maggie: *Thanks for the invite but I think we already have a table.*
> Rodney: *Cool. I will join you.*

"Oh Lord," Maggie said out loud.

"What?" Alex said.

"Rodney's joining us at wine night."

"Fine with me," Alex said. "I'll add him to our reservation."

Maggie found the contact image and selected Angie's cell number. Surprisingly, she answered on the second ring. Maggie chatted a few minutes before finally asking if they could all meet. She nodded her head a few times before hanging up.

"She'll meet us tonight at the casino," Maggie said, putting her phone down.

"Here we go," Britney said with a big smile.

CHAPTER 19

Strawberry Daiquiri

The casino was only twenty minutes from the compound so the girls decided to arrive early, have a few drinks, and feed the machines. The gaming floor was crowded and noisy. Maggie was not a big fan of crowds but followed Britney into the center of the action. She quickly pulled a Benjamin out of her pocketbook and slid it into a machine then started pushing buttons.

Maggie fished out a twenty-dollar bill and slid it into the machine next to Britney. Alex stood back and watched. Maggie pushed the button a few times until no more credits were left.

"That was fast."

Just then Britney's machine lit up, blasting all kinds of musical noises and attracting the attention from all those around her.

"You just won, fifteen hundred dollars," Alex said.

Maggie said, "Of course she did."

"I'm cashing out," Britney calmly announced. She pushed a button...The sound of money dropping into a tin can replaced the music. The dispensing of Britney's winnings went on for much too long, so Alex reached over and hit another button to stop it. The total showed, and a thin slip of paper came rolling out of a slot in the machine. Britney grabbed it and walked to the cashier's desk, holding the note proudly.

"Drinks on me," she said, coming back to the girls and holding fifteen crisp one hundred dollar bills.

"Let's go find Angie," Maggie said.

They found Angie dealing the high rollers at the $100 table. Her normal polite smile was strained, and her face was pale with dark circles under her eyes. She looked ten years older than she actually was. She spotted the three women, who hung back but watched the high stakes bets being made.

"Who can afford to play a hundred dollars at a time?" Maggie asked.

"That's the minimum bid." Alex nodded to one of the other players. "Take a look at the gentleman at the end, those aren't one hundred dollar chips, more like one *thousand* dollar chips, and he has a healthy stack in front of him."

"Look at all the players sitting there." Maggie watched the table incredulously. "Not one of them has just one chip."

"What if someone just came up and took one?" Britney said.

"There are cameras everywhere in this place," Alex explained, "they are *very* serious about their money."

"Damn, who are these guys?" Britney said. "We need to hang out here more often."

"I would bet most of the high rollers come from other countries," Alex said.

They continued to watch until Angie handed off her post to another very pretty dealer and signaled them to follow her. Maggie noticed two big guys—bouncers, she assumed—standing behind the card table, watching them closely as they left the high roller area.

"That was kind of intimidating," Maggie said.

"Yeah, don't let it bother you," Angie said as she joined them. "That's their job."

She led them into an open bar area, where she spotted a corner table away from any other patrons. She signaled the women to take a seat as she claimed the one closest to the wall, facing the door.

Angie ordered an iced tea. The other three women took Angie's recommendation of the strawberry daiquiris.

"They use real strawberries," Angie said. "It's more like a smoothie than a drink. I would have one, but I still have another session before the end of my shift."

"Do you get off the same time every night?" Alex asked.

"Pretty much, the weekends a little later." She winked at the girls. "Obviously, those are my best nights."

"The night Marco died, did you work a regular shift?" Maggie asked.

"We have this." Britney placed the gate report on the table before Angie had the chance to answer. Two lines were highlighted.

Angie coolly sipped her iced tea. "I told that detective, I was here until the end of my shift."

"Did you lend your car to anyone?" Alex asked.

Angie's face turned pale. "No, I didn't," she said in a low voice. She paused then turned to see who was sitting close by. Then she turned back to Alex. "It was Preston," she said. "He stole my car to get into the gate."

"Oh. My. God. Angie, did you tell the police?" Britney asked.

"Oh hell no. Preston would kill me. Plus, I'm sure he didn't kill my brother."

"How do you know?" Maggie asked.

"He told me," Angie said.

"And why would you believe him?" Britney said.

"He is an idiot, not a killer—*and* he said Marco was already dead when he got there. He had an extra set of keys that I didn't know about, but when the cops said I drove in twice, I knew exactly who took my car. When I asked Preston why he went there, he told me he went to steal my wedding ring; but he said he got out of there when he saw Marco lying on the floor, dead. He wouldn't have found the ring anyway. I was wearing it." Angie held up her left hand, displaying to the ladies a simple one diamond setting.

"But honestly," Angie continued, "the ring was not the reason he went there, it's not even real. I knew it was a fake diamond when he gave it to me. The gold is poor quality, I doubt he could get fifty bucks for it. I believe the real reason he went to Marco's that night was to either borrow money, or steal it. He definitely didn't want Marco dead: he was his only source of cash. He hasn't worked for over a year except for odd jobs Marco provided, which was mostly following people around or threatening them."

"Maybe he killed him by accident," Maggie said.

"I'm telling you, he didn't kill him. I'm one hundred percent positive," Angie said.

"Why are you wearing your wedding ring?" Britney asked.

"Keeps the weirdos to a minimum," Angie replied.

"Makes sense, I guess," Britney said. "But it seems like your tips might be bigger without it."

"Just the opposite, I'm afraid. I think most people, male or female, want what they can't have."

"What did the detective say about your car and the gate?" Alex asked.

"The police checked the security cameras at the casino; they showed I was at the table all night. I only took two breaks—and there's no way I could have driven all the way home and back in fifteen minutes. The cops are just assuming the club's bar code system is a piece of shit. They found several misreads," Angie said.

"Aren't there cameras in the casino parking lot?" Alex asked.

Angie nodded. "Yeah, but I park in the employee section behind the casino, and they only keep those recordings forty-eight hours. It's on a loop. The only time they might keep a recording is if there is an actual problem. But security always walks us out at the end of our shift. My car was right where I left it."

"Not really my business, but why are you still married to

Preston?" Alex asked.

"I don't have enough money to get a divorce." Angie shook her head in frustration. "Marco was going to help me pay a lawyer but kept putting it off until...well, you know."

"I actually saw Preston and Dale at O'Malley's last week," Britney put in. "They were so obnoxious they were eighty-sixed." She laughed. "You have to be really bad to get kicked out of O'Malley's."

"Those two are no good apart," Angie said, "but together they're definitely trouble. As a matter of fact, you won't believe the latest scheme they've come up with...."

"Do tell," Maggie encouraged.

"I have to get back to my table," Angie noted, "but the night Marco was killed, after the police left, I noticed Marco's desk was a mess. Normally it's stacked high but in an orderly fashion...Someone definitely went through my brother's desk and stole a life insurance policy."

"Are you sure?" Alex asked.

"Very sure, because I put it on top of the pile after I secretly made a copy."

Alex almost came out of her seat. "You have a copy?"

"Yeah, Marco told me he changed the beneficiary and said I would be happy. So I took it to work and made a copy then put it back before he knew it was gone. Now he's dead and I have no idea what to do about it."

Alex stared quietly into Angie's eyes. "I have an attorney who can handle everything."

"I don't have any money to pay a lawyer," Angie said, getting up from her seat.

"Don't worry about the money," Alex told her.

Angie nodded gratefully but said, "I really have to go. How about we meet at O'Malley's tomorrow when I can actually have a drink. I'll bring the policy, it's a lot of money."

"Definitely," Britney said. "How about five-ish?"

"Perfect." She polished off her iced tea then nodded to the three women. "See you ladies tomorrow."

The three women sat speechless, processing the information they had just heard.

*

As soon as Maggie got home from the casino she texted Detective Marker and waited for a response. Instead, her phone rang, and she quickly picked it up.

"What's up?" Mike asked.

"I think we figured out who killed Marco."

Maggie heard Mike sigh loudly. "Seriously, Maggie, I thought I told you to stop. Do you really want to end up in handcuffs?"

"Well, if that's what you're into detective…." She had said jokingly, but it came out sounding strange. Had she really just said that?

"Okay…" Mike paused to work through what she had just suggested before switching back to his professional mode. "Why don't you go ahead and tell me what you think you have."

"Angie told us that Marco had a life insurance policy—and guess who the beneficiary was?"

"Why don't you tell me?" Mike said.

"Angie," Maggie said excitedly. "She isn't divorced yet, so if Preston killed him, he would get half the money."

"That's not how life insurance works."

"What do you mean?" Maggie said. "Isn't Florida a fifty-fifty state?"

"Divorce laws are complicated; but what I do know is the proceeds of a life insurance policy go to the beneficiary, the spouse has no claim on it."

"Well, maybe Preston doesn't know that," Maggie suggested. "He is sort of an idiot."

"I'll look into it," Mike said after a moment, "but I have a pretty good gut instinct on these things, being a detective and all, and my gut says he didn't do it."

"Okay." Maggie was not going to argue with him any longer. "I just thought I would let you know what I found out."

"I'm going to tell you one last time," Mike said, letting out another loud sigh, "stay out of my investigation."

"If I find out something, by accident, you don't want me to tell you?"

"I would rather you don't find out anything...but if you do of course I want you to tell me. But no digging for it," Mike said, "do you understand?"

Maggie nodded, though she knew Mike could not see her. "I understand."

"Have you started your classes yet?" Mike asked.

His question caught Maggie by surprise. "What do mean? Or how did you know?"

"Good night, Maggie," he said. "Lock your doors."

"Good night, detective," she said. "I always lock my doors."

She hung up her phone.

Exhausted, she went into her room and changed into her sweats and a comfy shirt. Then she poured herself a glass of wine and turned on Netflix. But before she settled in she walked over to the front door and found it was indeed unlocked, so she flipped the lever.

"Jerk," she mumbled with a smile.

CHAPTER 20

Cosmopolitan

The pickle ball courts were the newest addition at the country club, so both courts were full most of the time, but the ladies took their chances and met up there. As they suspected, both courts were full, so they decided to sip the cosmos Fonzie had prepared for them in Styrofoam cups, while watching the oldies run the court.

"Angie is running late," Maggie said, looking down at her phone. "She'll meet us at O'Malley's at six."

"I wonder what that life insurance thing is about?" Britney asked.

"I can't wait to find out how much it's worth. I'll bet it's a million," Maggie said. "it's almost five now, should we go change?"

"I'm wearing what I have on," Britney said confidently, as she should have been. She was wearing a pink and white tennis dress that showed off her form perfectly. She also sported short socks and matching Nikes. Her hair was pulled back in a blond ponytail. She looked like Tennis Barbie.

"I'm wearing this," Maggie said, looking down at her black stretch shorts and an over-sized T-shirt. "It's just O'Malley's.

"Well, I'm changing," Alex said. "You girls wait here and I'll bring my car around and drive us."

"Sounds good to me," Maggie said.

Maggie and Britney watched Alexandra drive away on her cart. "Let's go to the bar," Britney said, "she's going to be a few minutes. We can get Fonzie to make us a 'to go.'"

"I just love that woman," Britney said, hopping into Maggie's cart.

"Me, too."

"Has she ever told you the story of 'the guy,' her first real love?"

Maggie shook her head. "No."

"It was a guy in New York, he was connected, if you know what I mean."

"Really?"

"He's the one who encouraged her to start her own business."

"When I first met her, she said she was a schoolteacher," Maggie said.

"That's what she told me too," Britney said. "I think she feels like people will treat her differently if they know how successful she really is or who her family is."

"Who *is* her family?" Maggie asked.

"I'm not sure, but they're also connected. When she got pregnant, her family pretty much disowned her."

"She always talks about her son," Maggie said, "I just assumed he was the biological child of her husband."

"The 'guy' is the son's father. She's never said his name. She always just refers to him as 'the guy.'"

"Interesting."

"Anyway, he broke up with her but made sure to keep an eye on her throughout her life."

"Why did he break up with her?"

"He was married and very high up in the 'organization.'"

Maggie frowned. "That sucks for her."

"Not really, because she met her husband Ira and had thirty amazing years before he died."

"Alex was actually nicknamed Mistress of the Mob," Maggie said, smiling.

"I can't believe she never told me any of that," Britney said. Then she pointed toward the cart barn. "Check that out."

Maggie stopped and pulled over. They watched as Alex and Fonzie stood face to face in the breezeway between the clubhouse and the cart barn. Alex was frantically waving her arms, Fonzie was backed up against the breezeway wall. Maggie couldn't hear the conversation, but it was definitely heated. However, it wasn't long before the altercation was over. The two women watched Fonzie disappear into the back door of the clubhouse, his head hanging low. Alex took off in her cart, never spotting Maggie and Britney.

"I wonder what that was all about?"

Maggie watched as Alex headed the opposite direction of her home.

"I've never seen Alex lose her cool, ever," Britney said.

"Yeah...something is definitely up," Maggie agreed.

When they reached the bar, Fonzie looked and acted perfectly normal.

"Two more cosmos, please," Britney said.

"To go?" Fonzie asked.

"Yeah," Maggie replied, "we're waiting for Alex." She watched as Fonzie flinched.

As Fonzie worked at the other end of the bar getting their drinks, Britney noticed he was wearing his shirt untucked. "Maggie," she whispered, "do you see that?"

"What?"

"The bulge," Britney said.

"Really, Britney?" Maggie chided.

"Oh my God, Maggie, gutterbrain. His waist," Britney said. "The bulge at his waist. I think he has a gun."

"No way, he's a bartender. He might even be illegal," Maggie said. "How would he get a gun?"

"We are in Florida; anyone can get a gun."

Maggie sighed, seeing Britney's point. "True."

Fonzie brought their drinks and set them down in front of

them. "Anything else, ladies?"

"Nope, thanks Fonz," Britney said. She grabbed both drinks and walked out the door, Maggie following, still in shock.

When Alex showed up to pick up the girls, she looked like a Fabergé egg. Diamonds and sapphires hung from her ears and encircled her fingers. Even her shoes had bling.

Maggie took a good look at her. "You know we're only going to O'Malley's?"

"One thing I've learned in my life," Alex said, "always present yourself in the best possible light. Now get in," she told them, "I'm dying to hear what Angie is going to tell us."

They arrived at O'Malley's a short while later. The parking lot had a lot of empty spaces, so Alex picked one right in front. There were also a lot of open tables, so they selected a high-top just inside the doors: they would still get the benefit of the air-conditioning but would be able to watch who came and went.

"What can I get you, ladies?" their server asked.

"Cosmo. Grey Goose, please," Maggie spoke first.

"Me too," Britney said.

Alex twirled her finger in the air.

"You got it," the server said. "Three Grey Goose cosmos."

"Nice car." Maggie pointed to the light grey and blue '55 Chevy parked under the tree at the far end of the parking lot.

"That's Dale's car," Britney said.

"Who's Dale?" Maggie asked. She thought she recognized the name.

"Preston's best friend," Britney said. "I'm surprised you haven't met him before. He's always around."

"If I saw him, I would probably remember," Maggie said.

Britney glanced around the bar, but she didn't see Dale sitting anywhere. "Unless he's in the bathroom, he's not here. What I can tell you is something isn't right. Dale would never park his car under that tree," Britney said.

Maggie again looked at the large tree in the corner of the parking lot. Its branches hung low, almost touching the hood and roof of the classic car.

"I just hope Preston doesn't show up," Alex said. "It seems like those two are always together lately."

"There's Angie now."

Alex pointed to the blue Honda pulling into the spot right next to Alex's car. They watched Angie park, grab her purse from the passenger seat, and get out of the car. She spotted the girls right away and waved as she started across the street.

Before she was halfway, a loud roar pierced the air and screeching tires seemed to appear from nowhere. Angie froze. Before she could move, the speeding truck ran right into her. It was as if she were a rag doll: she flew back toward the parking lot while the truck just kept going, disappearing around the corner before anyone could react.

Britney screamed. Maggie flew out of her chair, knocking over the server, who had their drinks on a tray but now watched them spill on the floor. A young woman ran over to Angie, screaming, "Call 911!" Alex, Britney, and Maggie watched in silent shock as the young woman announced herself as a paramedic and began shouting out orders to the crowd that had begun to form as she worked on Angie. After several minutes, the ambulance finally arrived, and the Boca police came in a swarm. The officers jumped out of their vehicles and formed a line, holding everyone back. Several took off around the corner where the truck had disappeared. Maggie saw one of the medics shake his head. Then the murmurs began to ripple through the crowd: the EMTs had pronounced Angie dead.

"There's her purse," Britney said, pointing to the large concrete planter just a few feet in front of them. "Should I go pick it up?"

"Do it, fast!" Alex said. She looked around; everyone was distracted by the commotion. "I can't believe this is happening," Maggie said, shaking her head. "I've never seen someone murdered before!"

"Me either," Britney said. She had returned with the purse; tears poured down her face. Alex reached for the purse and put it in her own. "We'll look at that later," Alex said.

Maggie put her arm around Britney. "Good idea."

As the women started to walk away from the scene, Britney turned back. "Oh my God, Dale's car is gone." She pointed to the far corner—and sure enough the '55 was gone.

"Okay, that's weird," Maggie said. "When did he leave?"

"I wonder if he had something to do with this?" Britney said.

"Of course he did," Alex said.

The police were busy stringing yellow tape around O'Malley's parking lot, and it looked as if they weren't going to leave; so the women decided to order more drinks.

"Maggie, call Wendy," Alex said.

"Shit, of course," Maggie said.

Maggie took out her phone and pushed her contact for Wendy, who actually answered on the first ring.

"Hey, Wendy, this is Maggie….No, we're still at O'Malley's….Well that's the thing, she was in an accident…wait…no, wait…I'm going to put you on speakerphone…" But Maggie didn't put Wendy on speakerphone; instead she stayed silent for a few minutes, obviously listening to whatever Wendy was saying. Finally, she said, "Wow, okay, talk to you later."

"What did she say?" Britney asked after Maggie had ended the call..

"Oh my God. You girls are not going to believe this."

"What?" Alex asked.

"She said that Preston definitely killed Angie." Maggie set her phone down in front of her. "She said it was the life insurance policy he found out about. He showed up at their apartment with Dale last night and he wanted some money but she refused. Then he said he knew about the life insurance and he expected half. She told him to go to hell, so Dale spoke up that if something happened to her, Preston would get the whole thing. Preston just smiled and told her to watch her back."

"Do you really think Preston is capable?" Britney asked.

"Preston might not be, but I have a feeling Dale was the mastermind. I heard he's been in jail for assault," Alex said.

"No way," Maggie said.

Alex nodded. "I heard he beat the crap out of some guy for sitting on his car."

"Seriously?"

"I was actually here that night. It was the Thursday night 'classics,' where the guys line up and drool all over each other's cars. Some guy leaned on Dale's car, and he told the guy to 'get the F off,' but the guy was drunk and jumped up and sat right down on the hood. I guess Dale grabbed him, threw him to the ground, and beat the holy shit out of him. The guy was in the hospital for weeks."

"There's a big difference between assault and murder," Britney said.

"There's a whole lot of money involved," Maggie returned. "Wendy said it was a million dollar policy."

"Oh shit," Britney said.

"What?" Maggie looked over to where Britney was staring and watched Detective Mike Marker climb out of an unmarked black sedan. "Oh shit is right."

"Well, hello ladies."

The detective had walked into the bar and approached the table where the women were sitting. Now he took the open seat they had saved for Angie.

"Detective," they all said in unison.

"Been here long?"

"Long enough," Alex said.

"Can you tell me what happened? It seems like you all had front row seats to the excitement tonight."

"You're not going to believe this," Maggie said.

"Try me."

Mike took the small notebook from his front pocket and waited for the girls to tell him everything they knew. They each took their turn reciting to the detective their version of what they had just seen, filling in for each other.

Maggie was in shock but recounted the conversation she had with Wendy. Mike listened but remained silent, writing everything down.

"Do you think Preston could have actually killed Angie?" Maggie asked the detective.

"I have no idea," Mike said, "but anything is possible." He closed his notebook and tucked his pen back in his jacket pocket. "You've been incredibly helpful, and I thank you for that."

"You're most welcome," Britney said.

They watched the detective move to the other side of the bar, speaking with other patrons who had witnessed the murder.

"What if it was just a hit-and-run...?" Britney shook her head, obviously still trying to process what just happened. "Or just an unfortunate accident...?"

"That is an incredibly naïve thing to say," Alex said.

"Do you think Preston killed Marco?" Maggie asked.

"Well, according to Angie, Preston found the life insurance policy after Marco was already dead, so what would be his motivation?"

"Angie was living with her brother, maybe Preston was mad about him taking her in?"

"Maybe," Alex said, "but I don't see it."

Just then they saw Mike look at his phone; the next moment he rushed out the door. He sprinted to his car and sped off.

"I wonder where he's going in such a hurry?" Maggie said.

The server nodded to Maggie as she set another round of drinks in front of them. "I heard one of the officers say they had Preston in custody."

Alex excused herself from the table. She went over to the tiki hut, which was currently absent of any smokers. She pulled her phone from her pocketbook and dialed. Maggie and Britney couldn't hear her words but her voice was elevated, as if she were giving orders. Whomever she was speaking to was on the butt end of the conversation.

When she returned to the table Alex looked worried but covered it with a wide smile.

"What was that all about?" Britney asked.

"We're having a manufacturing issue. Someone screwed up."

"I thought your plant was closed for two weeks?" Maggie said.

"It's our supplier, not my actual plant...but let's finish up, this has been a crazy night and I'm exhausted. Do you girls mind calling an Uber?"

"Not a problem," Britney said—and she and Maggie watched Alex rush out to her car. She climbed in quickly then squealed her wheels as she turned out of the parking lot.

"Something is definitely going on," Maggie said.

Britney nodded. "Let's get my car and go up to the club."

"Sounds like a plan; but it's after eight, nobody will be there."

"There might still be a few stragglers at the bar," Maggie said. But when they finally got to the clubhouse after going to Maggie's house to retrieve her car, the bar was closed.

"Shoot," Maggie said, "I wanted to talk to Fonzie."

"Well, there he goes." Britney pointed to a light blue Audi R8 pulling out of the parking lot. "No way a bartender can afford that car."

"Well, let's go," Maggie said.

"Where?"

"Wherever he's going."

CHAPTER 21

Amaretto Sour

The large iron gate of the oceanfront house opened slowly. Fonzie waited until the gate had opened wide enough to drive through.

"I'm going to have to follow him on foot," Maggie said.

"You're going to be trapped in there," Britney said. "I'll go with you."

"I need you out here in case something happens," Maggie said. "Just text me if you see anything out here."

"Okay, but be careful."

But Maggie had already jumped out of the car and was through the gate before it closed on her.

What are we doing here? Britney asked herself.

Maggie followed Fonzie down the short driveway. She waited behind a clump of palm trees until Fonzie climbed out of his car. She decided to take off her shoes so she could follow him along the travertine path.

Fonzie opened the trunk of the car and removed a briefcase. Then he walked down a path of multicolored pavers surrounded by exotic plants. Maggie followed, staying far enough behind so he wouldn't be able to see her if he turned around, but close enough to be certain she saw which door he entered through.

The door he approached was a tall double-framed door, at least eight feet in height, with long glass-frosted decorative windows. Fonzie pressed a few buttons on the lock: the door clicked open.

Maggie looked around but didn't see any cameras; still, she was careful to remain hidden by the lush landscaping as she quietly approached the house. The evening was too dark to really take it all in...Lights were coming on in the windows. She could see Fonzie moving through the house.

Maggie couldn't believe it. This could not possibly be Fonzie's house, but he was walking around inside it, stopping in the kitchen area to confidently pour what looked like Amaretto into a rocks glass. The furnishings looked high-end antique... Maggie knew the view must be spectacular. The whole front of the house faced the Atlantic Ocean. She could hear waves crashing on a bulkhead nearby.

This guy is the richest bartender in the world, she thought. The possibilities became unlimited in Maggie's mind: she imagined Fonzie as an international spy, or even something more nefarious, maybe a contract killer. As she went through the possibilities, she found herself a little disappointed. Fonzie was such a good bartender.

She continued to work her way around the house, avoiding the areas lit by tiki torches, finally reaching the back area. It looked like a resort. The swimming pool was hugely oversized. A giant rock waterfall rose above the deep end. A swim-up bar ran the length of one side. A lazy river snaked its way around the entire area. A large fire pit was lit up by recessed lighting built right into the apron of the pool; the fire pit was surrounded by at least ten chairs.

The sliders to the pool opened, and Fonzie stepped out. He had changed into a pair of shorts and a white short-sleeved button up that he left open: from the exotic lighting of the pool Maggie made out Fonzie's exposed chest, full of dark curly hair. He was carrying a glass half-filled with a golden brown liquid. He sat in one of the chairs in front of the fire pit and lit a cigar. He leaned back and put his feet up on the ledge of the pit.

Maggie took this moment to text Britney.

> Maggie: *I think this is his house. He's smoking a cigar.*
> Britney: *U OK?*
> Maggie: *Yeah. Just need more time.*
> Britney: *Be careful.*
> Maggie: *K*

Finally, Fonzie went back inside and the lights started to dim. Maggie felt safe enough to come out of the shadows and try the side door. The backyard was still lit up by tiki torches and a few accent lights. She needed to make it quick. She rushed past the sliders, hitting her pinky toe on a lounge chair. Her mouth opened wide but she held on to her pain, releasing only a silent scream. She continued limping to the door.

Fonzie had left it unlocked. Maggie opened it only far enough to squeeze through then closed it softly behind her. Immediately, she heard Latin music coming from the second floor. She looked around in amazement. The house was even bigger than it appeared from the outside.

Maggie took her phone out of her back pocket and selected Britney on FaceTime.

Britney's face appeared. "What is taking you so long?"

"Shhh! I'm in the house," Maggie whispered.

"Can you please get out of there," Britney said.

"Take a look at this."

Maggie flipped the phone around and did a slow, three-hundred-and-sixty-degree turn.

"Nice place," Britney whispered, "now get out."

Maggie spotted the briefcase that Fonzie had taken out of the trunk of the car. It was sitting at the end of the kitchen counter. She forgot about Britney and set the phone down next to the briefcase. She carefully placed the briefcase on its side and snapped the latches, releasing it. The noise was too loud; it echoed in the large space. She waited a few minutes until she felt safe to continue. Then she opened it.

There were several folders inside. The folder on top was labeled **BPR**. She opened it and turned through the pages. Contracts for the Boca Palms Resort.

The other folder contained a report in Spanish...or a report that seemed to be written in Spanish. It was *all* in Spanish. She put it back and shut the briefcase, snapping it as silently as she could.

Then she felt something cold against her head.

"Shit," she said aloud.

She slowly turned to face Fonzie.

"What the hell are you doing here, crazy bitch?" Fonzie said.

"'Crazy bitch'?" Maggie scoffed.

"What are you doing in my house?" he asked. He pointed the gun at her forehead.

"I followed you," Maggie said calmly. "By the way, nice house."

"It belongs to my family," Fonzie said. "But why would you trespass?"

"I don't know. Curious, I guess."

"You and your friends are way over your head. Now you have broken into my house"—he pressed the barrel of the gun to Maggie's forehead—"I could legally shoot you."

"*Are* you going to shoot me?" Maggie said.

"I don't know yet..."

"Shit," Maggie said.

"Come with me."

Fonzie grabbed Maggie's arm with his free hand while keeping the gun set close to her body. He led her into the garage, where he pulled some tie wraps out of a built-in drawer; then he pulled her back into the house. He sat her in a sturdy dining room chair and fastened her arms and legs securely to the arms and legs of the chair. Maggie watched him closely. A thought occurred to her. "Is your real name Miguel?" she asked.

"Yes," he said. "Now shut up, I need to think."

It finally hit Maggie, the situation wasn't good. Hopefully Britney wouldn't try to find her.

Fonzie pulled up one of the large chairs so he could sit facing Maggie.

"So why did you follow me here tonight?" he asked her.

"Rodney gave me a list of all the people who came in the gate the day Marco was murdered, so I was checking into everyone. You came in twice that day. Once at ten a.m. and once at ten p.m. The bar is closed at Boca midnight."

"Boca midnight?"

"Nine o'clock," she said. "You know, cause all the old people are asleep by then."

Fonzie just shook his head. "You people just don't exist in reality," he said.

"Did you kill Marco?" she asked. What did it matter at this point? she figured.

"It was an accident," Fonzie said shaking his head as if to get rid of the memory. "I went to confront him about something, and that crossbow was just sitting there, I picked it up and pointed at him—and it just went off. Shot straight through him."

"What were you going to confront him about?"

Fonzie scoffed lightly. "I had about ten million dollars' worth of questions..."

"He scammed you too?"

Fonzie shook his head. "No, someone I work for. He had the cash stashed somewhere, I wanted to know where and get it back. I definitely didn't want to kill him. He was worth much more alive than dead. I had to stick around to find out where the money was. I thought for sure he would have told his sister."

Maggie raised her eyebrow. "Did you kill Angie?"

"No," Fonzie said, again shaking his head. "I'm sure that was her idiot husband. I paid him to get anything he could from Marco's house, but as soon as he found that insurance policy, he saw his opportunity to cash in, and he forgot about me."

"So why did you stick around?"

"I was hoping you three amateurs would uncover something," he said.

"Why would we tell you?"

"You're at the bar every day talking about it," Fonzie said. "I'm not deaf."

"So now what are you going to do with me?"

"I don't know, yet." He pulled his phone out and sent a text. Maggie watched him.

"Who are you texting?"

"None of your business," Fonzie said.

"Fonzie," Maggie asked, "are you going to kill me?"

"I will if you keep calling me that."

"What? 'Fonzie'?"

"My name is Miguel, not Fonzie. Your girlfriend named me that when I first started, it's stupid."

"Sorry," Maggie said.

Fonzie stood up and took his phone out of his pocket again then turned away from Maggie.

"I have a problem," Fonzie said into the phone. He nodded, listening. "How long?...Shouldn't be a problem...Okay...See you in thirty minutes."

Fonzie took a small knife out of a drawer then slid the blade between the tie wraps around Maggie's wrists. He still held the gun in the other hand. Maggie rubbed her wrists one after the other while Fonzie undid the wraps around her ankles. Maggie decided not to do anything drastic.

"Let's go," Fonzie said.

"Where are we going?"

Fonzie smiled quietly at her. "It's a surprise."

He pushed her out the door and led her to the back of the car. Then he popped the trunk.

"Get in."

"I won't fit," Maggie said.

"Jesus, get in, *now*."

He pushed her as she tried to swing one leg in. Just then

Maggie heard a noise behind them.

"*Freeze!*"

Fonzie grabbed Maggie and spun her around, pushing her into whomever had come up behind them; then he took off around the garage.

"*Go!*" yelled a second voice.

Maggie stayed low on the ground. She rolled up into the fetal position, waiting for shots to be fired. But nothing happened. The next moment she felt a large hand on her back.

"Are you okay?" a familiar voice said.

Maggie slowly uncurled herself. She sat up and shook her head in disbelief.

"Silas…" she said. "How did you know I was here?"

Silas smiled and helped her to her feet. She wrapped her hands around his big shoulders and didn't want to let go.

"Britney called Jay. We got here as fast as we could," Silas said.

Jay appeared next to Silas, stepping from somewhere out of the darkness.

"He's gone," Jay said.

"Aren't you going to call it in? Are you cops?" Maggie suddenly asked.

"Not quite," Silas told her. "We work more on the private side."

"So, you're definitely not contractors?"

"Not the kind you're thinking," Silas said.

"But you're not cops, right?"

"Nope."

"Oh my God, so you slept with me for the job?"

"In all fairness, you put the moves on me."

"I certainly did not," Maggie insisted.

Jay sighed. "Come on," he said, "let's get you home."

They walked out of the gate then came over to where Silas had parked his truck next to Maggie's SUV. As soon as Britney saw them, she ran over and wrapped her arms around Maggie. They remained that way for several long moments, then

Britney pulled away. "You okay?" she asked. She held on to Maggie's shoulders and looked into her face.

"Yes," Maggie answered. "How did you know I was in trouble?"

"You left FaceTime on...I heard everything. But I had to finally hang up and call Jay." She shook her head. "I was *so* scared!"

"So was I," Maggie said. She felt her eyes grow moist but wiped the tears away before she lost total control. "Did you hear his confession?"

"No."

"How did you know to call Jay and not the police?"

"I knew Jay and Silas were spying on us," Britney said. "But not in a bad way."

Jay spoke up. "You knew?" he said.

Britney turned to him and winked. "Not my first rodeo, big boy."

"How long have you known?" Maggie asked her.

"Since the first night I met this guy." She pointed to Jay.

"And you still slept with him?"

"Um, sister, look at him...yeah!"

"All right ladies," Silas said, "let's go."

"Where are we going?"

"You're going home," Silas said.

"But don't you want to know what Fonzie told me?"

"Nope, got it all." Silas held up a small device.

"How?"

"I bugged your phone," he said.

"How?"

"I encrypted it when I was in your car."

"Oh my God, you *have* been spying on me!"

This time Silas winked. "It's my job."

Maggie looked from Silas to Britney and then back to Silas. "Where are the police? Didn't anyone call them?"

Silas shook his head.

"We can't call the police," Britney said.

"Why not?"

"Alex hired Fonzie," Britney said.

"I don't understand."

Now Maggie felt the tears falling down both her cheeks. Silas came over and wrapped his arms around her. She was tempted to melt into him but found her strength and pushed him aside.

"Wow," Maggie said, shaking her head.

Wiping her tears away she opened the door to her SUV and got behind the wheel. But she couldn't drive. Britney stood next to her.

"You can't drive," she said. "Get in the passenger seat."

Maggie climbed out of the car then climbed back in on other side. She settled down and fastened her seat belt. She could feel her hands start to shake so she clasped them together....She had just about been shoved into the trunk of a car, maybe even killed, and nobody seemed to care.

"You okay?" Britney said again.

She looked sideways at Maggie as she drove down the dark streets, following Silas's truck.

"Where are we going?" Maggie asked weakly. She just wanted to go home.

"I'm not sure where," Britney replied, "but we're meeting Alex."

CHAPTER 22

Last Call

It was the lights that woke Maggie from her trance; they were at the small airport in Boca. They parked next to Silas's truck and climbed out of the car. The guys signaled to Britney, indicating that she and Maggie should follow them to the only plane parked near the runway. Alex was just getting out of a black sedan. She saw her two friends and the two large men walking toward her. She walked over to them and wrapped her arms around Maggie.

"I'm so sorry, Maggie. The boys got there as soon as they could."

Maggie shook her head. "I'm just so confused..."

"I'm sure you ladies have a lot of questions," Alex said.

"A few—like..." Maggie pointed to the plane.

"Aw, yes, Jay and Silas both work for me. Private security."

"Does Fonzie work for you too?" Maggie asked.

"He does—or did." Alex shook her head. "I'm not really sure when things went wrong. I needed to keep an eye on Fonzie, but also on you two. I wanted to keep you safe."

"I slept with him," Maggie said, pointing to Silas.

"Good for you," Alex said, smiling. "He's a hunk."

"Did you have Marco killed?" Britney asked.

Alex turned to her. The expression in her eyes hardened.

"Absolutely not. Fonzie's job was to keep an eye on Marco and get my money back. After Marco died, he was going to leave after a reasonable amount of time to avoid suspicion."

"Did you know he killed Marco?" Maggie asked.

"I had my suspicions but he finally admitted it to me yesterday."

"Shouldn't we call the police and tell them?" Maggie asked.

Alex frowned. "It's no use. He's gone, he'll be out of the country within the hour."

"How?"

"He's a very resourceful man. The only person the police will arrest tonight is me. That's why I'm heading back to New York, where my attorneys can sort it all out. I had nothing to do with Marco's murder. I just didn't want my son to find out about my entanglements with Marco; so I set up a side business with him until he stabbed me in the back. I just wanted to get my money and get my hands on some important papers that tied me to Marco. He could have bankrupted my company."

"What about the life insurance policy?" Maggie said. "The premiums were being paid by your company...."

"Yes, but we put that together as a protection. The first year, we made a huge profit, so we reinvested, but I wanted to make sure if something happened to him, I could get my money back. The company was worth over ten million dollars after less than a year. I had no idea we would be so successful. Since I had made Marco a full partner, he was able to assign his sister as the beneficiary to his shares. It was supposed to be paid to the company—which was me. Changing it was just his last shot at me for wanting to liquidate the company and go our separate ways."

"You didn't tell us," Britney said.

"I love you girls and I didn't want anything to happen to you." She drew closer and embraced them. "I have to go, but I would appreciate you ladies keeping this to yourselves tonight. I need a bit of a head start."

"I'm not telling anyone," Britney said.

"Why don't you call the detective tomorrow, Maggie?" Alex said.

"Why?" Maggie asked.

"They're going to find out anyway, you may as well be the one to tell. Maybe you could get a date out of it." She smiled then walked to her plane.

Maggie and Britney watched her go. The guys climbed aboard, waving as the door closed. The girls stood back by their car; they did not climb in until the plane lifted from the ground.

"This is all too unbelievable," Maggie said.

"Anything is possible in this town," Britney replied. "Believe me, I've lived here my whole life."

*

Britney drove into her driveway and got out of the car. Maggie got out and hugged Britney before getting into the driver's seat.

"Do you think I should call the detective?" Maggie asked.

Britney shrugged. "She said to, so yeah."

Britney waited at the front door until Maggie drove down the street. She went into her house then directly to her closet. She pushed the code into the keypad until she heard the click. The door released. She had converted the spare bedroom into a closet just to hold her shoes and bags. The walls were lined with racks and specialized hangers. The lighting was motion sensitive: as soon as she walked in, each of the shelves illuminated, highlighting the specific shoe or bag lying there with highly filtered bulbs that would not affect the colors or deteriorate the fabrics. A large crystal chandelier hung right above a large velvet round bench that she had designed for the room.

As she did often, she stood for a moment, admiring her creation. She had imagined this room since she was a child. Her imagination was what gave her the motivation to design high-end lobbies.

She walked over to the signed Amy Burnett painting of a woman in a large hat. She pulled at the painting. It slid aside to expose a small wall safe. She pushed several numbers in sequence until the safe unlocked. She carefully placed the small notebook that she had recovered from Marco's place in the back of the safe, behind several stacks of money and a few jewelry boxes. She placed the cell phone Jay retrieved from Fonzie's house, next to the notebook. She would eventually give it back to Maggie, but she didn't want her to be tempted to call anyone tonight.

*

Alex sat back in her seat and opened the *Palm Beach Post*. A photograph of Preston Parker, being led away in handcuffs, took up half the front page. Alex read the caption. Preston was being charged with the murder of his estranged wife, Angie.

"What a shame," Alex said aloud. "Let's see how long you last in prison."

Alex had used the young man a few times for certain errands. He was reliable most of the time; however, when she sent him to Marco, he was supposed to keep her informed. He had turned out to be more unreliable than she foresaw…and she was fairly certain Marco figured it out. He had given Preston false information that he would pass on to her.

Those boys had no idea who they were dealing with.

She folded the paper back in half and closed her eyes. Tomorrow shit was going to hit the fan; she would need to be well rested. Her lawyers were already on standby, and the plant was opening on Monday. So her return was justified. She would deny any knowledge of Fonzie's background. There was no law against hiring an investigator. Maggie would confirm his confession: she had it recorded on Maggie's phone, which would be returned tomorrow.

*

Maggie awoke the next morning, thinking she had heard a knock on the door. She tied on her bathrobe then hurried to the front door and opened it. No one was there—but a plastic Publix bag was hanging from her doorknob. She pulled off the bag and closed the door. Her phone was inside the bag…but it was dead.

She plugged it in then got in the shower.

When she was fully dressed and had drunk a good cup of coffee, she took the semi-charged phone to the back patio and sent a text to the detective.

> Maggie: *I know who killed Marco.*
> Mike: *Seriously Maggie? It's Sunday and I'm tired.*
> Maggie: *I'm not kidding. It was Fonzie and he tried to put me in the trunk of his car.*
> Mike: *Very funny.*
> Maggie: *I am not kidding, please come over.*
> Mike: *On my way.*

Mike was there before Maggie finished her coffee. She told him everything that had happened, making sure to downplay Alex's involvement.

"How did they find you?" he asked.

"Silas bugged my phone," she said.

"Let me see it."

Mike reached for her phone. He swiped a few times then tapped when he found the app he was looking for. He played back the recording of Fonzie. Then he seemed to resume swiping and tapping. Maggie watched quietly.

"Everything else is erased," Mike said. "Who had your phone?"

"I don't know. I left it on the counter at Fonzie's."

"Okay." Mike nodded. "Well, I'm taking it for evidence."

He pulled a plastic bag from his pocket.

Maggie blinked. "Seriously?"

"You can go get a new phone," Mike suggested.

"Is Alex in trouble?" Maggie asked.

"I don't know, but we definitely need to talk to her."

Maggie tried to deflect the conversation. "I wonder what Marco did with all the money?"

"This is going to sound crazy," Mike said, "but a lot of it went to care for his mother."

"What?" She stared at the detective in disbelief.

"She's in a very expensive home in upstate New York. A place that specializes in Alzheimer's."

"Wow." Maggie shook her head. "Did Angie know?"

"Yes. That's the reason for the life insurance policy, he wanted to make sure if something happened to him, Angie could keep paying for it."

Maggie stared at Mike uncertainly. "Is Marco a good guy or a bad guy?" she said.

"It seems like both," Mike replied.

His phone was buzzing, and he pulled it from his pocket. He looked at the screen and immediately went pale.

"What is it?" Maggie asked.

"My sister," he said. "I have to go."

Maggie walked him to the door. "I hope everything is alright," she said as he walked away.

He turned back to her and said, "Zoey's mom is dead." Then he climbed into his car and drove off.

Authors Note

Hope you enjoyed BEHIND THE GATES. This is a work of fiction. Names, characters, businesses, places, events, locales, and incidents are either the products of the author's imagination or used in a fictitious manner. Any resemblance to actual persons, living or dead, or actual events is purely coincidental.

~~The~~ Kay

The Sun begins its setting... Callum sighs and notes the fading waves. He paddles 'slowly' to shore... not trying the never ending tide for view of Buddy's waiting - yup. "Buddy" "I'm coming" Buddy frantically frolickes in the unusual tide... desperation in his yelps to travel, see his owner. Callum 'stoically' steps out of the Atlantic... like it's his last steps or Buddy goes crazy! "Yup, Buddy- I hear you - you big dope" he addresses the dog.

d to his right — St Ives! ah, at it's best - the light - my god - no wonder everyone wants to be here...